B♏

D0882265

SPECIAL MESSAGE TO READERS

This book is published under the auspices of

THE ULVERSCROFT FOUNDATION

(registered charity No. 264873 UK)

Established in 1972 to provide funds for research, diagnosis and treatment of eye diseases. Examples of contributions made are: —

A Children's Assessment Unit at Moorfield's Hospital, London.

•

Twin operating theatres at the Western Ophthalmic Hospital, London.

•

A Chair of Ophthalmology at the Royal Australian College of Ophthalmologists.

•

The Ulverscroft Children's Eye Unit at the Great Ormond Street Hospital For Sick Children, London.

You can help further the work of the Foundation by making a donation or leaving a legacy. Every contribution, no matter how small, is received with gratitude. Please write for details to:

**THE ULVERSCROFT FOUNDATION,
The Green, Bradgate Road, Anstey,
Leicester LE7 7FU, England.
Telephone: (0116) 236 4325**

In Australia write to:
**THE ULVERSCROFT FOUNDATION,
c/o The Royal Australian and New Zealand
College of Ophthalmologists,
94-98 Chalmers Street, Surry Hills,
N.S.W. 2010, Australia**

A RECKONING AT ORPHAN CREEK

When Sandy Wakefield, Flint's uncle, dies in a mining mishap, Flint and Johnny Wakefield suspect foul play. Sandy was trying to improve the miners' lot, who work long hours in dangerous conditions for a pittance. Then, Flint and Johnny discover the stripped body of an unknown man and seek to learn his identity. But life above ground gets as dangerous as below. Ultimately, it seems, Flint will have to die before there can be a reckoning at Orphan Creek!

*Books by Terrell L. Bowers
in the Linford Western Library:*

A BATTLE AT LOST MESA
THE GUNS AT THREE FORKS
WARRICK'S BATTLE

Ward County Public Library

TERRELL L. BOWERS

A RECKONING AT ORPHAN CREEK

DISCARDED

Complete and Unabridged

LINFORD
Leicester

First published in Great Britain in 2008 by
Robert Hale Limited
London

First Linford Edition
published 2009
by arrangement with
Robert Hale Limited
London

The moral right of the author has been asserted

Copyright © 2008 by Terrell L. Bowers
All rights reserved

British Library CIP Data

Bowers, Terrell L.
   A reckoning at Orphan Creek .—
   Large print ed.—
   Linford western library
   1. Western stories
   2. Large type books
   I. Title
   823.9'14 [F]

   ISBN 978–1–84782–583–4

Published by
F. A. Thorpe (Publishing)
Anstey, Leicestershire

Set by Words & Graphics Ltd.
Anstey, Leicestershire
Printed and bound in Great Britain by
T. J. International Ltd., Padstow, Cornwall

This book is printed on acid-free paper

1

The sweltering heat deep within the earth's bowels produced an endless stream of sweat that soaked a man's shirt and matted his hair until it was a soggy wet mop. The dust boiled about the drill spewing about like a penetrating steam, so thick the man on the hammer could hardly see to strike without hitting the bit-man's steady hand.

'We about there?' Sandy Wakefield asked, pausing to set down the eight-pound double-jack. He knelt down on one knee to rest and waved a hand in front of his face to clear the cloud of powdery haze.

Todd Shelby paused to wipe the back of a gnarled hand along his forehead to prevent the beaded perspiration from trickling into his eyes. Then he put his thumb on the bit, flush against the rock wall for a measurement and removed it from the bored hole. He held it out so they could gauge the depth.

'Looks like we need another two or three inches yet.' Shelby paused to cough, his body doing its best to reject the build-up of dust in his lungs. The clearing of one's throat was so commonplace among the miners that no one thought much about it. Every man working underground hacked up dirt-wads of phlegm from breathing in an endless supply of dust. He regained his wind and sighed. 'I swear getting ore out of this old gal is 'bout as hard as pulling rattlesnake fangs.'

'You kin say that again, Shel. Durn slow going having to blast every inch of the way. This here is the most stubborn stone I ever come across, and I been a hard-rock stiff fer twenty years. Tackling a mountain like this is enough to turn a man into a farmer.'

'It'd be a might easier if our bit weren't completely worn out,' Shelby observed, running his finger over the drill tip. 'Time to toss this one in the scrap heap.'

'Yep, and this hammer is so rounded on one side I can't use it 'cept to pound rock. We shore'nuff need to buy new tools.'

'No argument from me there, Sandy.'

'Another week until the first of the month. Then we get us another couple bits and a new double-jack,' Sandy remarked. He paused to show his few remaining teeth in a grin. 'Howsome-whatsoever, if you was to ask, I'm sure old man Talbot would be glad to charge a hammer and a new bit to your account.'

'Thanks a bunch,' Shelby grunted sourly. 'But I barely take home enough to break even as it is. I reckon when I die, I'll end up owing my soul to that damn company.'

'Yeah, tell me the story, pard. I ain't got no kids or wife to support, and I can scarcely scratch enough coins for beer and a couple hands of cards.'

Shelby chuckled. 'You'd have money

a'plenty if you were able to ever win at cards. You are without a doubt the worst card player I ever run across. If I didn't have a healthy dose of conscience, I'd sit down with you every payday and clean you out.'

Sandy laughed in return. 'Good thing for me that you have such a strong constitution about — ' He stopped in mid-sentence, listening intently. The smile vanished, replaced by an instant alarm.

Shelby's head turned as well. The same sound reached his ears — the hiss of a burning fuse!

'Fer the love of — ' Sandy yelled. 'Fire in the hole!'

'Get out!' Shelby shouted back, throwing down the drill and trying to get his feet under him. 'Get out of here — quick!'

A mighty concussion shook the earth. Flying stone, debris, and a wall of dirt spewed forth from the explosion. Great chunks of rock crashed down to fill the dead-end tunnel. Shelby and Sandy had no chance to escape. Both men were trapped inside, buried beneath tons of rubble.

Beyond the smoke and billowing dust, a miner cried out, 'Cave in!' Several men began to holler back and forth for help. Miners came rushing in the direction of the explosion from other stopes and chambers. There had been no warning, no one had been prepared for the blast.

As the dust began to settle, miners with picks and shovels scrambled over the debris, sifting through the thick haze, searching for the victims of the explosion.

'Vot happened?' Big Swede's voice silenced the chatter and confusion of the miners. 'Tell me, who be blasting without giving us due warning?'

'I think it's the tunnel Shelby was working in,' Weasel answered. 'Him and Sandy were down on this end.'

'Ain't no way those two would fire a short or bad fuse,' Pepper Jones avowed. 'They were the best among us at setting dynamite.'

'It don' matter the why of how it happen,' Big Swede growled. 'Bring da slag carts down here. We got to dig them out. Hurry! There's a chance they may still be alive.'

The miners began working furiously, but their hopes were not high. If a man was not crushed outright in such a blast, he could survive only a few minutes buried under a ton of rock and debris. From the outward appearance of the wall of crumbled rock, it was going to take hours to reach the two miners. Even as they began working furiously to dig them out, each man knew that the chance of finding Shelby or Sandy alive was very slim.

* * *

Flint Wakefield was doing his daily studying when his father opened the door and poked his head into the room. It was obvious that something was wrong. Boyd never interrupted him during his studies.

'Come into the sitting room, Flint,' the man said quietly.

It mattered not that Flint was a grown man of twenty-four, he seldom questioned an order given by his father. He set his book aside and followed after Boyd.

A foreboding seeped into his being at seeing his younger brother and sister both sitting on the stuffed leather couch. Mother Wakefield was also there, her face impassive, telling nothing. Whenever Boyd had the floor, no one else spoke up or interrupted. The same as Flint, his mother and the other members of the Wakefield family always respected Judge Boyd Wakefield's assuming authority.

'A telegraph message arrived a few minutes ago,' Boyd began. 'Pete, from down at the train depot, brought it up as soon as it arrived.' He took a deep breath and let it out slowly. 'I'm afraid it's bad news.'

'Has something happened to Doc?' Johnny broke the silence. 'Is he all right?'

Flint flashed him a look of annoyance. His younger brother had jumped without thinking. All his query did was slow down the process of discovering what this was all about.

'Nothing concerning your older brother,' Boyd gave his question a satisfactory answer. 'The last word from Doherty was the letter we received from him a couple weeks ago.'

Flint noticed that his mother sighed with relief, evidence that Boyd had called everyone together without telling her the news.

'Seems there has been a cave-in over at Orphan Creek,' the head of the household continued. He paused and lowered his head, sorrow bowing his wide shoulders. 'Sid and another man were killed.'

Flint experienced an emptiness that spread throughout his chest and his stomach rolled into a knot. It had been a couple of years since Flint had seen his uncle, but the man had always brought laughter and sunshine with his infrequent visits. He was a jovial sort, with a ready wit and quick, toothy smile. Sid — or Sandy, as the old boy preferred to be called — had been carefree, jolly, a real character. He had chosen not to take a wife and put down roots like Boyd. Instead, he passed through life like a tumbleweed, blowing from here to there, going wherever the breeze took him.

'That's a real shame,' Flint said quietly.

Timony, the youngest of the Wakefield clan, bobbed her head in agreement with him. 'Yes. Even though Uncle Sid was not around a great deal, I've always felt that he was part of our family.'

'We were practically two buttons on the same suit as kids,' Boyd responded gravely. 'It wasn't until I started my law practice that he began to roam about on his own.'

'Going to be dull without him coming to visit any more,' Johnny put in. 'We've grown up with stories of you and him, and what a pair of wild hellions you were as kids.'

Flint marvelled that Johnny could say something like that and get a smile out of Boyd. He would have expected a tongue-lashing for not showing respect. As was often the case in many families, his father was inclined to be soft toward both his younger brother and sister — the babies of the family.

'We had a few scrapes,' Boyd admitted. 'It was a wild and untamed land back then. I can tell you that, whenever Sid was around, there was never a dull moment.'

'Anything we can do?' Flint offered.

Boyd stepped over next to his wife and placed a hand on her shoulder. Her natural response was to place her hand over his own. It was the way they were, a team, as smooth in unison as any pair of matched horses in harness.

'We would like to pay our respects but, with my bad back and your mother's rheumatism, neither of us could endure such a hard trip. Orphan Creek is too far away and practically inaccessible for a carriage.'

'As I recall, it's about sixty miles this side of Leadville,' Flint thought aloud.

Boyd gave his head a nod. 'And built into some of the tallest, steepest mountains that Colorado has to offer. If ever a man was rugged, it had to be the joker who decided to try and mine that region.'

'When is the funeral?' Flint asked.

'The telegram stated it would be held in the next day or so.'

'If I leave within the hour I might make it in time,' Flint suggested.

'Count me in,' Johnny was quick to add. 'I'm coming too.'

'So will I,' Timony joined in with her brothers. At Flint's sharp glance, 'I can ride circles around either Flint or Johnny.'

'This ain't no chore for a girl!' Johnny told her curtly.

'I ain't no girl, I'm a full-growed woman!' Timony snapped right back.

Boyd held up a hand to silence the Wakefield children. Then he chose to speak first to his daughter. 'Your mother needs you here, Timony. She

11

promised to host the house-raising for Mrs Freedman's son and new bride. She can't feed twenty or thirty hungry men by herself.'

Timony's petite features worked into a frown. 'I'd rather go to a funeral.'

'Think of all the guys who will be there,' Johnny teased. 'You can let them think that you actually know how to cook. They'll be lining up at our door to court you.'

'I'm not looking for anyone to court me just yet, Johnny. Next year, I am going to attend either Smith College or that new one, Radcliffe, back in Massachusetts. I want a formal education and then I'm going to get a job teaching. Unlike you, I want to do something with my life.'

'An educated woman is about as much fun to have around as a pocketful of cactus,' Johnny scoffed. 'Besides, isn't one of the requirements to get into a college to have a brain?'

'I did a lot better in school than you did, Johnny.'

'Oh, yeah? So how many buckets of shucks does it take to fill a wishing well?'

'You can be so childish sometimes,' Timony said . . . and stuck out her tongue at her brother.

Flint cleared his throat to prevent further bickering between the two. 'I'll need some expense money for room and board, plus Sid may have left some debts behind.'

'We have some cash stowed away here in the house,' Boyd assured him. 'I'll make sure you have enough for everything.'

'I'll throw some things together and get started,' Flint said. 'With any luck, I can catch a ride on the lower loop of the Denver and Rio Grande railroad and take the train to the stop nearest Orphan Creek. I should be there by tomorrow afternoon.'

'Hey, I'm going too!' Johnny insisted.

'I can manage it alone,' Flint said quickly. 'I can travel quicker without you tagging along.'

'Pa!' Johnny turned to Boyd for help. 'I liked Sid, too. He was my uncle, same as he was to Flint. If he goes to Orphan Creek, I ought to be able to go as well.'

'Little brother, you are nothing but a walking headache,' Flint struck back. 'Every time we go any place together, you get us into some kind of trouble.'

'This a funeral, not a Fourth of July celebration,' Johnny pointed out. 'We only had a run-in over at Glenwood Springs because those cowboys were drinking and bragging about how tough they were.'

'Yeah, and I'm the one who ended up in the fight.'

Johnny grinned. 'What with Doc back East studying medicine, you are the big brother in the family: it's your job to be the toughest.'

Boyd again held up a hand for silence. 'There's no time for argument. The two of you can ride out as soon as you are ready. Mother will put together a few supplies and I'll give both of you some money for whatever expenses

14

might come up.'

'But, Pa!' Flint pleaded. 'You know that turning Johnny loose is like putting a fox in a houseful of chickens. I guarantee he'll find a way to get us into trouble.'

Boyd took on the scowl of the Honourable Judge Wakefield. 'It'll be up to you to keep him out of trouble, Flint. You two pay our respects and make sure Sid didn't die owing money to anyone. We Wakefields always pay our debts.'

Flint sighed in defeat. Once his father had made up his mind the argument was over. 'All right, Pa, I'll make sure everything is taken care of.'

'The fun-loving old wart,' Boyd said, his voice cracking with a cherished recollection. 'I'm going to miss his ornery hide.'

'I'll fix the two of you some sandwiches for the trip, while Mother readies the supplies,' Timony offered, resigned to remaining behind.

Boyd put a narrow look on Flint.

'Remember, you boys mind your own business. I don't want you to get mixed up in any trouble.'

'You're telling me?' Flint showed total innocence.

'I remember the last time I sent you on an errand to Grand Valley — and that was without Johnny. You ended up in the middle of a range war.'

'It was nothing more than an honest mistake,' Flint said, flashing a disarming grin.

His father was not so easily pacified. 'That one mistake could have cost you your life. If I hadn't been able to pull some strings, you might have ended up busting rocks in a territorial prison. As you will soon be an attorney-at-law, you have to admit something like that isn't the kind of résumé to attract job offers from the railroad or major corporations.'

'I didn't intend to get involved in a full-scale war, Pa. All I did was stop a couple of hardcases from beating some guy to death. The next thing I know, people are taking up sides and the war is on. I only helped to stop the fighting.'

'Yeah,' Johnny gibed, 'by shooting two of the hardcase gunnies working for the other side in a gunfight.'

'You've always been too gifted with your fists and guns,' Boyd backed up Johnny. 'I rue the day I gave you that Frontier Colt.'

'We're going to a funeral this time, Pa. If anyone gets us into trouble, you can bet it will be Johnny's doing, not mine.'

Their father gave a bob of his head at the comment but sighed. 'I'll take heart in remembering those words.'

⋆　⋆　⋆

Lavera Shelby's head was lowered shamefully, but she stood erect, shoulders squared. She hated the thought of working at the tavern, serving drinks, obligated to listen to foul talk and crass jokes, forced to ward off advances and dodge hands from pawing drunks.

'I'm offering you a good job, Lavera,' Henry Talbot announced, like he was king. In essence, he did sit on the throne and decide the fate of everyone in Orphan Creek. He gave a dismissive wave of his hand. 'And don't be fretting about what anyone will think. The miners all knew and respected your father. No one is going to think ill of you for working tables here. This is a respectable job.'

Respectable, she reflected dolefully, working in a saloon, a bar, a casino, a tavern — whatever the name, they all stewed in the same kettle. She had never had any respect for the women who worked in such places!

'Lavera,' Talbot said, 'I like the sound of your name. It is unique, rather like a star performer with a theatre group.'

'It was my grandmother's first name,' she explained quietly, wondering what Grandmother or Mother would think of one of their offspring working in a tavern — paid to serve drinks and wait tables, all the while trying to avoid being coerced to sit or drink with men who gambled and drank away their meagre wages.

'You can earn extra money here,' Talbot was saying, subtly glancing her over from head to foot with an all too familiar gaze. 'Pretty thing like you, every man in camp will want to buy you a drink.'

'You said the job was only to be a waitress.'

He shrugged his shoulders. 'No one is suggesting you do more than sit down and keep a man company for a few minutes. If a fellow buys you a drink, you earn half the price of your own drink.'

'I don't intend to take up drinking.'

Talbot smiled. 'You wouldn't be drinking liquor or beer.'

'Then — '

'The miners don't know what's in your glass,' Talbot explained quickly. 'The bartender fills your glass with tea. We charge the miner for a whiskey and half of that goes into your pocket. Some of the girls who work here earn an extra five or even ten dollars a week by being a little sociable.'

Lavera gave her head a negative shake. 'I'm not prepared to sit with customers.'

'Well, suit yourself,' Talbot gave in. 'But a waitress doesn't earn but four-bits a night, plus tips. You should know that most of these miners don't waste their money on gratuity.'

'I understand.'

'Excuse my being curious, sweet-heart, but how do you intend to pay your rent and provide food for your family on four or five dollars a week?'

'Shane is working at the Dingo mine moving slag. Between us, we'll get by.'

'A clean-up boy and a waitress,' Talbot said, shaking his head. 'I fear you are both going to starve.'

'We wouldn't be the first,' Lavera retorted, unable to keep the bitterness from entering her voice. 'The Fraizer family lost two of their children to the cold and hunger last winter, when Ben was hurt and unable to work. I know of many others too.'

'I sympathize over the loss of anyone's loved one, but accidents and hard times are not my fault.'

'Whose fault is it?'

Talbot gave his shoulder a careless shrug. 'These are simple miners, Lavera. Most of them don't plan a single day ahead. They spend their money as fast as they earn it. If they would put something away each month, then they would be prepared for an emergency or injury. I keep telling them, but they don't listen.'

'You know full well that the family men don't have any money left at the end of the month. The high cost of rent for housing, for fuel, and the excessive prices you charge at the store keeps everyone broke.'

Talbot set his teeth and a dark hue flooded his complexion. 'Implying I am some sort of shyster is not the way to get hired for a job, young lady. Do you want to work here or not?'

Lavera acquiesced, lowering both her eyes and her voice. 'I do,' she murmured.

'Then, when it comes to criticizing me or the other mine owners, you would do well to keep your opinions to yourself. If I were a ruthless man, I could kick you out of your cabin and rent it to another able-bodied miner and his family. There is a long waiting list for housing and I'm sure to have a number of enquiries concerning your cabin. If you give me a hard time you and both of your brothers will end up sleeping out under the stars. Do I make myself understood?'

Lavera swallowed her pride. The job offered was the only one available. If she didn't work, it was a certainty that her family would be put into the streets. With winter only weeks away, such a consequence could easily mean a death sentence.

'Yes.'

'Yes what?' Talbot asked in a harsh tone.

'Yes, Mr Talbot,' Lavera replied meekly.

Talbot seemed satisfied with the dressing down and was once again amiable. 'You know I'm a bachelor, Lavera,' he said easily. 'There are alternatives to working long hours and never having a dime to spend.'

Lavera felt her heart grow heavy and a knot twisted in her stomach. 'I'm sure I don't know what you mean.'

A wry smile played upon his lips. 'Let's not be too innocent, pretty one, we are both adults here.' He raised his eyebrows in a coercing arch. 'A little sociability can go a long way, if you are friendly to the right people.'

The lewd insinuation pumped life back into her constitution. 'I am not a lady of the evening, Mr Talbot! My favours are not for sale — not for any price!'

He appeared amused at her rebuke. 'You can start tomorrow night,' he said, as if the subject had never been brought up. 'Be here promptly at six o'clock.

Cracker will tell you when you can leave each night.'

Lavera gave him a curt nod and left the tavern. As she walked toward the long row of houses, she felt a heavy weight upon her shoulders. Her father had been strong and self-assured. She had never worried about going hungry, or being thrown out into the cold world empty-handed. With him laid out alongside Sandy Wakefield and scheduled for burial that next afternoon, her world had turned dark and was filled with gloom.

She weighed her options and found no alternatives to working for Talbot. Shane was too young to go into the mines. As clean-up boy, he earned a few dollars a month. Grant Shelby, the youngest in the family, was not yet old enough to enter the workforce. With this job she would be home until Shane finished work, so someone would always be around for Grant. Being the eldest, the responsibility for their future was on her shoulders. She had to

Ward County Public Library

provide for the three of them, even if it meant discarding her principles.

Lavera knew there was a second alternative: she could marry one of the miners. There were no less than a dozen suitors chasing after her to do exactly that. Two of them were very nice young men, both honest and hard-working, but . . .

I won't be a widow at thirty! she vowed.

The life of a miner or his wife was not a pleasant prospect. They worked six days a week, ten hours each day, and came home worn to a frazzle and covered in grime. Then it took most of their earnings for rent of a one-room company shack and the buying of supplies from a company store that charged excessively high prices. What kind of life was it to be forever broke and hungry? And scratching out a scant living continued only as long as her husband was lucky enough to not end up permanently crippled or killed in the mines.

No, she would not allow herself to fall in love with a miner, nor would she auction off her favours to a disgusting lowlife such as Talbot. She would make do until the boys were grown. In two years' time Shane could work in the mines, or get a job somewhere else. Another couple of years after that and Grant would be ready to seek out a job and be on his own.

Lavera stopped on the path and looked up at the cemetery on the hill. Her father would soon be resting among those unfortunate souls. Her primary concern had to be survival. She would do what was necessary to keep a roof over the heads of herself and her brothers. If that meant serving drinks in a smoke-filled tavern, while dodging the attentions of half-drunk miners all night, then that's what she would do.

2

Orphan Creek was nestled within the shadow of several towering peaks from the Sawatch Mountain Range of Colorado. Flint had never figured out where the Sawatch Mountains separated from South Park, or where South Park ended and the Middle Park began. To him, every mountain range looked about the same as the last, from the San Juans in southern Colorado to the North Park range on the southern tip of the Wyoming border. It was easier to consider all of the different ranges as part of the Rocky Mountains and let it go at that. One thing he was sure of, the ride up to Orphan Creek was not a ride he would have wanted to make in the stormy winter months.

Upon entering town, Flint observed the usual businesses he had seen in other mining towns. One side of the road boasted a large company store, a two-storey building which was a tavern or saloon, and a blacksmith-livery combination at the far end of the main street in town. On the opposite side were a small freight office which had a sign reading POST for mail, a jail house and a couple of sizeable houses. Beyond the limited services of the heart of town were a dozen rows of company-owned one- and two-room shacks. Upon the slopes, there were some tents, a few covered wagons and two buildings which resembled bunkhouses. Near the edge of town were railroad tracks which led to dump chutes for loading ore cars. There were also a number of worn paths leading back into the hills from the dump sites.

As he and Johnny rode slowly along the main street, Flint noted a gathering of people on the slope of one hill. It did not take a close examination to make out a number of wooden crosses that marked the local cemetery.

'Looks like we almost got here too

late,' Johnny spoke up, also taking notice of the throng of people.

'The funeral must be in progress,' Flint agreed.

They continued toward the crowd, until they reached a place to dismount. Flint and Johnny climbed down and tied off their horses, before the two of them solemnly walked over to join the mournful group. One of the men was reading from the Good Book. He paused briefly to survey the newcomers, but did not cease his recitation of the scriptures.

The Wakefield brothers stopped, removed their hats and ducked their heads, as the man speaking began a prayer for the dearly departed. It was short, reverent and to the point.

'Amen,' he finished. 'Rest in peace, Sandy Wakefield and Todd Shelby, you will both be sorely missed on this here earth.'

Flint said an 'Amen' and placed his hat back onto his head. Johnny followed suit. The gathering began to break up, but one man appeared to take a special interest in them. He walked their direction, regarding both him and Johnny with cautious, constantly shifting eyes.

'I'm Bullet Skinner,' he introduced himself curtly. 'You boys got business in Orphan Creek?'

Flint immediately disliked the man's belligerent attitude. It was Johnny, however, who spoke up.

'And what concern is it of yours?' he asked impudently. 'You some kind of welcome wagon hostess?'

Bullet rotated his head to the side and spat a stream of tobacco juice into the dirt. 'I'm town marshal and head of security for the United Mine Owners of Orphan Creek,' he stated importantly. 'Anyone entering town is my business.'

'Good enough,' Flint spoke cordially, before Johnny could make another smart reply. 'You're probably the man we need to see.'

'Yeah?'

'I'm Flint Wakefield, Sid's nephew.

This is my brother, Johnny. We got word that Sid had been killed and came to see that he was properly laid to rest. Can you tell us what happened?'

'Some guy named Sid?'

'You probably knew him as Sandy. He preferred that name to Sid most of the time.'

'Sure, I knew Sandy. He and Todd Shelby were killed in a cave-in,' Bullet informed them matter-of-factly. 'It was an accident.'

'What kind of accident?'

'Seems your uncle and another miner had a faulty fuse on a powder charge. It went off before they were ready. Brought a ton of earth down on top of them.'

'My Uncle Sid ... Sandy,' he corrected, 'he always told us over and again how a miner had to be real careful.' Flint studied the man for any reaction. 'I can't tell you the number of stories he told us about the wrong or right way to deal with explosives. It's hard to believe he would get himself

31

killed by way of a stupid mistake.'

Bullet's shifty eyes flicked from him to Johnny. His voice was strong, but there was an underlying hesitancy to his words. 'Well, that looks to be the way it happened, Wakefield.'

'No witnesses?'

Bullet spat a stream of juice again. 'No, and I don't want anyone poking their nose into things that don't concern them. I talked to the men at the mine and I'm telling you it was an accident.'

'All right, Marshal, we'll take your word for it.'

'I put your uncle's things in a box. He didn't have much in the way of possessions. You'll find it over at the livery.'

'We'll pick it up later.'

'Good,' Bullet snorted. 'I don't like loose ends.'

'You don't mind if we stick around a day or two?'

'What for?'

'Oh, you know, to make certain

Sandy didn't owe any debts, maybe put a nice marker on his grave, that sort of thing.'

The muscles in Bullet Skinner's jaw worked. It was obvious he didn't want the two new arrivals to stick around, but he had no grounds for ordering them out of town. He rolled the chaw from one cheek to the other and paused to spit again. 'Suit yourself, boys,' he said at last. 'Just stay out of trouble.'

'We are law-abiding citizens, Marshal,' Flint said with the utmost respect.

Bullet bobbed his head and sauntered away, his big shoulders swaying back and forth with each step.

'You smell something'?' Johnny asked, as soon as the man was out of earshot.

'Man didn't seem eager to become fast friends, did he?'

'I remember Sandy telling us about the ins and outs of handling of explosives too, Flint. He must have told us a hundred different stories about men who were killed or had lost body parts due to being careless. He always called those guys stupid and sloppy. He wouldn't make a greenhorn mistake with an explosive charge.'

'I agree, but it might not have been his mistake. The marshal said he was working with another man. Maybe it was the other fellow who was at fault.'

'So what's our next move?'

'I intend to ask a few questions about the second man, just to be certain in my own mind this was an accident.'

'Sounds like a good idea to me.'

They waited until the crowd had dispersed before they walked over to the two fresh graves. There were a few wild flowers placed at the head of both mounds of dirt. The names of the two deceased had each been painted on a wooden cross.

'Rest in peace, Sandy,' Flint murmured under his breath. 'Dad and the rest of us are going to miss you.'

'So long, Uncle Sandy,' Johnny added.

'Durn shame.' A man's deep, rich baritone voice spoke up from behind them. Flint turned his head to see a slender black man. His face shone with a sincere regret.

'Were you one of Sandy's friends?'

'I don't know of no one what weren't a friend of his. Sandy was about as right as a spring rain. Many a time he would lend a hand with firewood or stop by with the makings for a meal for a family down on their luck. He was one of a kind.'

'How about the other guy?'

The man's sad expression did not change. 'Todd Shelby was a hard-working Christian man, too. He done had three kids depending on him. It's going to be durn tough on them.'

'Doesn't the mine take care of widows and orphans?'

'They usually give the survivors a *'here's a few dollars — now git'* send-off. Being naturally big-hearted, they don't toss them out of the company-rented cabin for at least a day or two. We miners donate whatever we can — which ain't much. I recollect one miner's widow last year left here with little more than the clothes on her back.'

Flint frowned. 'That doesn't speak very well of the mine owners.'

'Henry Talbot pretty much tells the other two mine owners what to do. He controls the biggest mine, the tavern and company store. The other two are mostly concerned with the operation of their mines. They all live by the same rule — so long as you are able to work, they are happy to keep you on the payroll. Get injured or sick, you end up depending on your friends for your keep.'

'Even if you are injured on the job?'

'Don't pay for a man to get careless.'

'That hardly seems fair.'

The man grinned without humour. 'Fair ain't what working these here mines is all about. We miners were only put on this here earth to make the mine owners rich.'

'Were you in the mine when the accident happened?' Johnny wanted to know.

'I was up another tunnel. All I heard was the explosion. Don't know that anyone else was working down next to Sandy or Todd.'

'This Shelby fellow,' Flint asked, 'he new at handling explosives?'

'Not him. Between those two fellows, they had thirty years of experience. I can't imagine either of them making the mistake of lighting a short or quick fuse.'

Flint changed the conversation. 'Is there someone in town able to carve a proper headstone? We'd like something special to mark Sandy's grave.'

'The blacksmith is my cousin. He does most every kind of carpenter work, or welding. I 'spect he would be the one to talk to.'

'Appreciate the information, Mr — I didn't catch your name.'

'Pepper Jones.'

'Well, thank you, Pepper Jones,' Flint told him. 'I'm Flint Wakefield, from over Colorado Springs way. This is my brother, Johnny.'

The three shook hands, then Flint bade the man farewell. Watching him walk back toward the rows of company houses, he was struck by a bad feeling. He felt the need to finish their chore and get away from the mining community as quickly as possible.

'That smell is getting worse,' Johnny said. 'You think maybe someone wanted to be rid of either Sandy, or that Shelby fellow?'

'I don't know,' Flint replied honestly. 'I find it hard to believe anyone would have reason to want Sandy dead.'

'What do you want to do next?'

'Guess we ought to head over to the livery and talk to the blacksmith about that headstone.'

'Don't take two of us to do that,' Johnny told him. 'How about I wander down and see if Sandy owed any money to the company store?'

'All right, but stay out of trouble.'

'Hey, I'm only going to ask about his bill, OK?'

Flint hated to let his younger brother

out of his sight, but there was no reason to worry about him going to the store. What could happen?

He took both horses and went down to the livery. The blacksmith might have been Pepper Jones's cousin, but there was no similarity between them. Pepper was as lean as a bronco buster, while Fudge Jones was a squat, powerfully built man. With a scowl on his face, he would have been a man to whom to give a wide birth. However, he displayed an easy-going nature that put any apprehension to rest.

'Yep, me and Pepper started roaming right after the end of the War for Freedom between the Union and the Confederacy. We were in the army for a time chasing hostile Indians and kind of kept moving west. He picked himself up a wife a few years back and I found my Maisy a while after that. We lighted here right after Excalibur went into operation. Me, I don't like being closed in, so I landed this top-side job.'

'I see a lot of tools and iron lying about.'

'You kin ask me to make about anything and I'll do it,' he said without really bragging. 'I started working with a forge and welding when I helped tend to wagons and horseflesh for the Union cavalry. The old smith who taught me was as good as they come.'

'It has to be better working up here on the surface than down in the mines.'

'You ain't telling me nothing I don't know to be true. I spend a good part of my time sharpening drill bits. I know some blacksmiths work right down in the mines, but not me. The miners give me their drills at the end of their shift and I sharpen them so they are ready by morning.'

'Then you must work some late hours?'

'I can put a good point and edge on a drill in no time at all. I'm usually cleaned up by nine or ten o'clock.'

'What about a nice headstone of some kind for my uncle?'

'I've the tools to carve with and I have a slab of sandstone that I had brought in for that very purpose. It'll take me a couple days but I can do it.'

'That should be fine — Fudge, was it?'

He grinned. 'Real name is Marrol. I hated it.'

'Where did the handle *Fudge* come from?'

'When I worked at my first army post, the livery was right next to a house of worship. I was in the habit of using some unfavourable language until then. The parson asked if I would please find a few other terms that wouldn't offend his flock. I began saying 'fudge' instead of swearing. Pretty soon, everyone started calling me the 'fudge man'. It kind of stuck and I liked it a whole lot better than Marrol.'

'The marshal said he left my uncle's things here.'

Fudge went over to a corner and dragged a crate over to Flint. There wasn't much of anything worthwhile

— ragged clothes, a broken American Waltham watch, a few loose coins and a worn, yellow-tinted, keepsake photograph of Sarah Bernhardt.

'The Divine Sarah,' Flint said, recalling a term he had heard linked to her name. 'I recall reading how she has toured much of the United States. Sandy never even saw her on stage. He only picked up this photograph from some Frenchman — won it in a card game.'

'Must have been the only time in his life that he ever won,' Fudge remarked. 'That there fellow never knew when to bluff or fold. He belonged at a poker table like I would a knitting bee.'

Flint went through the remainder of Sandy's things. He had a worn notebook, but the only items written on the pad were the addresses for Doherty and Boyd Wakefield. It was odd he would be communicating with Doc, what with him away at school. Maybe the oldest son of the family had a special place in their uncle's heart.

There was nothing else of value or interest in the man's belongings; not much to show for a man's life. It proved his own evaluation of the man had been correct, Sandy had lived like a tumbleweed blowing about in the wind.

Finished with the unhappy chore, Flint outlined what he wanted on the tombstone with Fudge, shook the big man's hand and began walking toward the main buildings in town.

★　★　★

Johnny ventured into the company store and found several customers. He took some time looking around while the people paid or signed for their purchases. The place was well stocked with just about anything a person could want: a combination bakery, pharmacy, clothing and food store. However, the exorbitant prices were at least three times what he usually paid for the same merchandise elsewhere. He supposed it was due to shipping the goods up a narrow mountain trail, but it still seemed awfully expensive.

The last customer, other than for himself, was a young boy. Johnny could not help hearing the exchange between the kid and the storekeeper.

'I can't go home empty-handed, Mr Gates. My little sister has got to have some milk or she'll die!'

'It ain't my fault, Davy, I can't help you,' the man told him firmly. 'Your pa ain't worked a lick in three weeks. You've reached the limit on your credit. I can't let you have a single grain of salt without you first getting the OK from Coup Jacobs. Your pa works for him and he is the one who sets the limit for his employees. I'm sorry, but that's the way it is.'

'My father ain't able to walk yet, Mr Gates,' the boy said quietly. 'And Ma is down sick with a fever and don't have no milk. The baby is going to starve, if we don't get something in her right sudden.'

'I'm sure Coup or Mr Talbot will do

something for you, Davy. But without their say-so, I can't do anything about extending more credit to your family. It isn't me — I'm only following the company rules.'

Another man entered the store. He looked about Flint's age, dressed in buckskin breeches and vest, with stringy blond hair hanging down to his shoulders. He strutted into the place with the arrogance of a barnyard rooster. He surveyed the store and swaggered over to the counter, his hand resting on the butt of a pearl-handled gun, which was tied low on his hip. Tipping his head to the side, he glanced down at the boy with disdain and turned to the storekeeper.

'What's the problem here, Gates?' he asked haughtily.

'No problem, Sparks. Davy was just leaving.'

Sparks put an insolent gaze on the kid. 'There's the door, young Cren-shaw. Careful that it don't hit you on the backside on your way out.'

'I can't go home without some milk,' the boy replied stubbornly. 'There ain't no way to feed the baby. She's been crying from hunger for hours.'

Sparks grabbed the boy by the ear and pulled him forward. 'Gates told you to beat it, pup!' He followed the words by spinning the boy toward the door and giving him a swift kick in the seat of the pants. 'Now get!'

Johnny strode forward and tapped Sparks on the shoulder. 'Take it easy there, fellow,' he said. 'You don't have to boot a boy around like that.'

Sparks whirled about, placed a hand on Johnny's chest and gave him a shove. 'Back off, bucko!' he snarled. 'You mess with me and I'll — '

Johnny did not reply in words, but lowered his head and charged into Sparks, driving him right out the door. The two of them went off the porch and landed on the dusty street in a tangle of arms and legs.

Johnny was almost as big as the blond man, but he was not as experienced. A solid boot caught him in the ribs and knocked him rolling. Before he could get to his feet, a fist exploded in his eye. He was knocked onto his back, stunned and momentarily helpless.

Sparks scrambled to his feet, standing over the dazed Wakefield. He drew back a foot to kick him in the head —

Flint had almost reached the store, when a young boy was shoved out the door. Moving a step closer and two bodies flew out the door. He groaned at recognizing Johnny as one of the combatants. 'I swear,' he muttered to himself, 'that kid could get into trouble at the blessing of a newborn baby!'

Seeing the blond gent was getting the best of his brother, he rushed forward. When the guy got to his feet and drew back to take a swipe at his Johnny with his foot, Flint slammed into him with his shoulder. The violent contact sent the blond man reeling. He was knocked two steps to the porch, bounced off the store wall and sat down hard. His shock and surprise immediately turned to fury.

'You shouldn't have butted in, stranger!' He snarled the words.

'That's my brother, tough guy,' Flint replied. 'You pick a fight with him, you pick a fight with me.'

'Let it go, Sparks!' the storekeeper said from the doorway. 'There's been no harm to his point!'

But Sparks jumped to his feet and came at Flint with his fists raised. Flint, however, was not as green at fisticuffs as Johnny. He let Sparks close to within striking distance. When the man threw a hard roundhouse punch, Flint batted the man's guard to one side and countered with a solid right to his jaw. The insolence fled the man's expression instantly. He took the full brunt of the blow and staggered a step back. A pulverizing left to his stomach and a second right to his head sent him back another step. Before he could catch or steady himself, Flint hammered him flush to the chin a second time and sent him sprawling into the street on his back.

'Smart thing for you is to stay there and think about this for a minute,' Flint cautioned him, panting to catch his breath. The higher elevation had sapped his air until he was already winded from the short exchange. He paused to point a warning finger at the man. 'If you get up I might have to hurt you, fella. Myself, I don't like fighting; it's childish and makes people bleed.'

Sparks sat up and spat a mouthful of blood into the street. 'Yeah,' he mumbled dismally, 'I see what you mean.'

Flint waited as the man slowly got to his feet, but Sparks had obviously lost interest in continuing the altercation. He staggered away on shaky legs, wobbling off down the street.

'You pack some punch,' a youngster said from nearby, his eyes wide with wonder and admiration. 'I never seen anyone knocked flat any quicker than that before.'

'Fighting is a sign of immaturity,' Flint told the boy, while staring straight at Johnny. 'Some people never grow up.'

'He was sticking up for me,' the boy came to Johnny's defence. 'Sparks didn't have to throw me out of the store.'

'So my little brother decided to do something about it.'

'Yep.'

Johnny grinned, while gingerly fingering the swelling under his eye. 'Don't know why you joined in, Flint. I was doing all right.'

'Yeah, I recognized your usual strategy — wear him down beating on you.'

'I was lulling him into getting over-confident,' Johnny argued. 'Then I would have nailed him like a wall plank.'

'You can't stay out of trouble for five minutes, can you?'

'I didn't know I was working to a time limit, big brother,' Johnny answered, getting to his feet and beginning to dust himself off.

Flint shifted his attention to the boy. 'So what started all the trouble, sonny?'

'My pa got his leg banged up in a mining accident a while back and can't get around yet. My mom is down sick, or she would have come to ask for what we need.'

'Then what's the problem?'

'We owe a debt here at the store, so Mr Gates can't give us any more credit without Mr Jacobs or Mr Talbot's saying so.'

'And who are they?'

'Mr Jacobs owns the Dingo mine, where my pa works; Mr Talbot owns the store.'

'And the mine owners don't help out a man who is injured on the job,' he stated, remembering his previous conversation.

'That sure ain't happened around here yet,' the boy agreed.

Flint took the boy by his shoulder and marched him back into the store. He stopped at the counter and addressed the man named Gates. 'I'd like for you to give this young fellow what he needs.'

'This ain't none of your business, stranger!' Gates complained. 'This is a company store and company business. I can't give him any credit unless my boss, or his father's employer, gives me the OK.'

'I've heard a little about company stores before,' Flint replied. 'The mine owners provide the store, then charge whatever they like to the miners. With no competition, you pretty much charge whatever you like.'

'You ought to check the prices on the stuff in here,' Johnny said from behind Flint. 'Must be triple what it should cost.'

Gates glowered at him. 'Mr Talbot sets the prices. I only run the store. I'd suggest you get out of here — both of you — before the marshal shows up!'

'I met him already,' Flint said easily. 'He seems a fair man.'

'That was before you hammered one of his deputies senseless, stranger. If you're smart, you'll listen to me. I'm only trying to save you from getting yourself busted up or thrown into the local jail.'

Flint held up a hand to stop the man from continuing. 'We don't need to involve the honourable marshal, Gates. You give this young lad whatever he needs and I'll pay you cash for it. That's fair enough, isn't it?'

The change in the storekeeper was like magic. He revolved instantly from sour and obstinate to blatantly obsequious. 'Well, yes, certainly!' He fashioned a smile. 'That's very generous of you, stranger.'

'I don't know if I can let you do that,' the boy protested. 'We Crenshaws don't beg from strangers.'

Flint cast a sidelong glance at him. 'Your pa can pay me back once he is back to work. It isn't charity, it's a loan.'

He frowned. 'I guess that would be OK, you loaning us the money.'

'I'll see to this, Flint,' Johnny spoke

up, placing a hand on the boy's shoulder. 'Do you happen to have an older sister, sonny?'

'Meg,' Davy replied. 'She is doing laundry to help pay for our rent.'

'Must be a fine young lady, huh?'

'Naw, she's just my sister. Thinks she's all grown up, but she's only sixteen.'

'Might be worth a look,' Johnny said, winking at Flint. 'How about I help you pick out a few things, Davy. We'll take them over to your house together.'

Flint put his hands on his hips. 'Johnny, if you get — '

'It's no problem, big brother,' he said, grinning. 'I'll be sure and get myself an invite to supper. You're always complaining that I'm underfoot. Well, now I won't be.'

'I made arrangements with Fudge Jones for us to sleep at the livery.'

'You sure do spoil us,' Johnny simpered. 'The refreshing smell of horse leavings, acrid smoke from a smouldering forge, with mice, crickets and spiders crawling over our blankets all night . . . sounds real nice.'

Flint set his teeth. 'I don't want you getting into any more trouble.'

'Me?' Johnny feigned innocence. 'Trouble?'

Flint watched his brother lead the boy down an aisle, picking out several items. He decided that he was wasting his time worrying. His brother was too old to watch over like a toddler. He put his attention back on the storekeeper.

'What about Sid . . . Sandy Wakefield?' he corrected. 'Did my uncle leave this world owing any money here at the store?'

'I don't recall Sandy ever charging a cent, but I'll take a look.' Gates removed a book from under the counter and thumbed through a few pages. He stopped at the name Sandy Wakefield, ran a finger down a column of figures, and shook his head.

'Sandy was square. He never spent more than he earned. Really will miss the old boy. He was a good guy.'

'Know of anyone else he might have owed money to?'

'Possibly at the tavern, but I kind of doubt it. Like I said, he was not the kind of guy who liked to run up an account.'

Flint thanked the man and asked, 'Can you tell me which place belongs to the Shelby family?'

Gates thought for a moment. 'Fifth house, third row up the hill, but they won't be home. I remember someone saying there was going to be a dinner for the kids, something of an after-funeral wake.'

'Guess I can wait to speak to them.'

'The eldest is Lavera Shelby. If you miss her at the house, my wife was telling me she heard the girl is going to work at Talbot's Tavern starting tonight.'

'I'm obliged.'

'Real pretty gal, Lavera,' Gates said. 'Shame about her pa dying along with your uncle. Todd was a popular guy, never heard a bad word about him. He always paid his bill on time too. We're going to miss both of those fellows.'

'You said a man named Talbot sets the prices here?'

'Henry Talbot, he owns the tavern, the store and the Excalibur, the first mine started up in these hills. He's the man who named this place Orphan Creek, after the little stream that runs just over the first rise.'

'We crossed it coming into town.'

Gates looked around and lowered his voice to a whisper. 'Talbot charges me fifty per cent on everything I sell. I have to add on enough to live, so it makes prices awfully high. Like I told you, it isn't me.'

'I've been around mining towns and company stores before, Gates. I hear what you're saying.'

'I'd have given Davy the milk he needed, but one word of charity and I'd be sent packing. Talbot keeps close tabs on my inventory and sales. I wouldn't dare cheat him and don't dare give anything away. I'm too old to work in the mines. This is the best job I could get . . . both for me and my wife.'

Flint gave a nod of understanding and checked on his brother. Johnny was still helping Davy with his shopping, so he decided to let him pay for the stuff himself. He still wanted to do a little checking around. Accidents happened all the time in the mining industry, the constant danger was part of the job. His concern was only to verify this had been an accident!

3

The tavern was referred to as the Company House and catered to three different mining crews. Coup Jacobs owned the Dingo mine, Spinner King owned the High Grade mine, and Talbot was the king of the hill. He not only owned the largest and most productive of the three mines, he owned the company store and the only tavern in town. There were Dutch, German, Italian, Cornish, Welsh, and a few Negroes and Mexicans in the assortment of miners. Irish were intentionally excluded from the trio of mines at Orphan Creek. Even before the violence and mayhem associated with the Molly Maguires, a good many mine owners looked upon the Irish as undesirables and criminals.

Within the confines of the Company House, several of the different ethnic bands gathered in individual groups. Smoke drifted from cheap cigars and rolled cigarettes, the smell mixed with that of cheap liquor and sweat. At some tables, men spoke in their native tongue and reminisced of homelands or loved ones left behind. Some would gamble, while others were there to pass the boredom of their lonely existence. All shared living under the shadow of death, one that followed them into the mine each working day. Bandages were wrapped about skinned knuckles, arms or heads, while other men hobbled on damaged feet, ankles or legs. Their jobs were as rough and hazardous as any the country had to offer.

Lavera could understand the need of such men to release their fears and energies in strong drink. Her father had often told her that the brawling, gambling, singing, or dancing was simply a way to let off steam, a manner of forgetting that any single night might be a man's last on earth. However, she had never thought about such men having so little patience. Everyone wanted their drink or service immediately. Talbot enjoyed thinking of himself as being fashionable and offered a menu of drinks that were similar and easily confused. Men could order anything from a mint julep, to a host of *do* drinks — fancy do, mixed do, peach, racehorse, cherry, strawberry and claret do. He also had oddly named drinks like knicker-bocker, pig and whistle, floater, and a host of others.

While most men ordered ale, a foamy brew, or whiskey, some delighted in asking for phlegmcutter, tog, rot-gut or red-eye. It was soon apparent that a few jokesters were trying to fluster her as a form of entertainment. She was glad for the miners who had worked with her father at the Excalibur, as they took pity on her and kept their drinks simple.

After running herself ragged for a solid two hours, she began to have some understanding of the other two girls working with her that night. Each of them would serve a few drinks, then sit down with one or more of the miners and have a drink herself. Not only did the girl earn half the price of her own drink, she could rest from the hurry-up rush of serving the other tables. It made her wonder if her pride was worth the extra effort.

Scolding herself for allowing her aching legs and feet to take command over her good sense, she discovered a solitary figure at the back of the room. He was sitting alone, quietly patient, a man who did not fit into the mining community in the least. While every miner old enough to have facial hair sported a moustache or beard of some kind, the gentleman was clean-shaven. Instead of grubby and patched denim, he wore a charcoal suit and spotless white shirt. His was not a miner's cap, but a fashionable flat-crowned Stetson. He was dark of hair and eyes, with an aquiline nose and resolute jawline. She sighed inwardly, mustered a pleasant look to her face, and walked in his direction. If he was a travelling drummer, perhaps he would leave her a tip — something she had not yet managed from the tight-fisted miners.

'I hope you haven't been waiting long,' she said, forcing a courtesy smile of greeting. 'It's rather dark back in this corner. I didn't see you until just now.'

'You must be Lavera Shelby,' he replied intimately.

That caused her to wrinkle her brow and instill a harshness in her tone of voice. 'How do you happen to know that?'

Flint immediately flashed a disarming smile. 'My uncle was Sandy Wakefield.'

'Oh!' she said, her expression instantly softening. 'Please excuse my being abrupt. I thought you were . . . ' She appeared to search for the right words. 'Anyway,' she evidently decided against comment, 'I'm sorry for snapping at you.'

'I've noticed that the other girls are allowed to sit with customers. Can I have a few moments of your time?'

Lavera gave her head a vigorous

shake. 'No. It would — the other men might think that I would also sit and have drinks with them.'

'I understand.'

'What do you want from me?'

Rather than answer her question, he tipped his head in the direction of the kitchen. 'I see a menu on the wall beside the bar mirror. Is there a cook available this late?'

'You want something to eat?'

'This is the only place in town,' Flint answered. 'My brother scrounged a meal with one of the miner families, but I didn't manage an invite.'

'Tell me what you would like and I'll see if the cook is still preparing meals.'

'One other thing, if you don't mind,' he said. 'Would you check and see if my uncle owes any money here. I would like to settle his account.'

'I'll ask Cracker,' she said, tipping her head toward the man who was working behind the long oak bar.

'Thank you, Miss Shelby. I would appreciate it.'

He ordered the meal and Lavera hurried toward the man she had called Cracker. Flint discreetly admired her walk, as it caused her skirt to rock to and fro. Having spoken to her, he knew it was a natural feminine gait, not an exaggerated motion to attract a man's attention. Even as he continued to keep an eye on her, she glanced back his direction then quickly looked away.

Flint smiled inwardly at the demure conduct. First impressions were often wrong, but the little nymph reminded him of a pert and frisky colt. There was fire in her animated eyes, bespeaking of an unbridled spirit, yet she was visibly bound with the morals and self-regard of a proper young lady. A wisp of auburn hair dangled down between her radiant, aqua-green eyes. She brushed impatiently at the strand and hastened to take an order from another table.

A figure appeared at the door and a sullen hush fell over the room. It took only a moment before Flint took notice of the man. When their eyes met, he knew that he was the one for whom Bullet Skinner was searching. The marshal strode through the maze of miners, skulking his way back to where Flint was sitting.

'You didn't waste any time getting into trouble, Wakefield,' he said thickly, planting himself across from the table like a man readying himself for a fight. 'Sparks works for me. It don't look good, having someone beat the snot out of one of my deputies.'

Bullet had evidently come looking for an excuse to exercise his authority. To neutralize the situation, Flint offered the man a gregarious simper. 'We were only exchanging views, Marshal. He thought my brother needed to have his head caved in with a boot. I have felt the same way a time or two, but didn't think it was his decision to make.'

'I told you not to start any trouble,' Bullet growled, not placated by the attempted humour.

'It won't happen again.'

The marshal was puffed up like the

swamp's biggest bull frog, but Flint had refused to accept his challenge. In an effort to exert his power one last time, he folded his arms and said pointedly, 'This is the last warning, Wakefield. I run this camp and I don't put up with troublemakers.'

'I hear you,' Flint replied evenly. 'From now on, I'll try and keep a tighter rein on my kid brother.'

Bullet paused to take out a licorice stick, took a bite, then took a plug of tobacco and also gnawed off a chaw. He gave a couple of chews to mix the blend, then shifted the wad to one side of his mouth and positioned it between his cheek and gum.

'You're gonna be more trouble,' he said thickly. 'I can feel it, sure as I'm standing here.'

'I never go looking for trouble, Marshal.'

The man gave him one last scowl, pivoted around, and stomped back out of the tavern.

As if the door closing was a signal for

celebration, the chatter and noise in the room instantly returned to normal.

Lavera arrived with a plate of food a few minutes later. She placed it in front of Flint and locked eyes with him momentarily.

'Your uncle never ran up a bill here. Cracker says he had a habit of losing money whenever he played cards, but he never borrowed from anyone or charged a debt of any kind.'

'I'm obliged to you for finding that out.'

'Anything else?'

'I would still like to speak to you privately.'

'I told you I don't — '

'About your father,' he silenced her objection. 'It won't take but a few minutes.' Offering up his most pleasant smile, 'I promise.'

'This is my first night working here. I'm not sure what time they'll let me leave.'

'I don't mind waiting. How about I walk you home?'

'That wouldn't be proper. I don't even know you.'

'Lot of miners drinking in here; what if one of them decides to wait for you and get friendly?'

'I can take care of myself.'

'All right, maybe I could come by your house tomorrow sometime. Would that be better?'

She hesitated, shielding her eyes with lash-adorned lids. 'I suppose so, as long as it concerns my father.'

'You worried about a jealous beau?'

The girl looked up at once. 'Beau?'

'Yeah, boyfriend, suitor, that sort of thing.'

There was a slight upward curl to her lips. 'I haven't heard anyone speak of having a beau since we left Saint Louis. I was just a little girl at the time.'

'How 'bout another round of drinks here!' a man bellowed from a nearby table. 'I'm buying a toast to Todd Shelby and Sandy Wakefield.'

Flint saw the fond memory fade from the girl's face. She was jolted back to the cruel world of working tables. 'Excuse me,' she murmured.

'What time tomorrow?' he asked, before she could leave.

'Let's make it around noon,' she said, as she hurried off to take an order from the man who had offered the toast.

Flint returned to eating, but the steak on his plate had obviously come from between the horns of a grey-bearded bull. He had to chew for ten minutes to get a single drop of juice. The fried spuds were raw in the centres and the beer was warm. He concluded that even a buzzard would have had lean pickings off of his plate. The meal had been listed as the Dollar Special. The only thing special about it was having the patron end up stuck paying a dollar for something he couldn't eat.

When he had chewed until his jaw ached and managed but two or three bites, he stood up from the table. He dug out a dollar for the 'special' and left an extra four-bits next to the plate. He would call it a night and resolved then and there to make other arrangements for eating the next day.

★ ★ ★

'There they are,' Bullet said, pointing out the window. 'That's Flint Wakefield and his brother. Looks like they are going up to your mine, Mr Talbot.'

'The guy dresses like a dude,' Talbot observed. 'He doesn't look like a fighting man.'

'Knocked two of Sparks' front teeth loose. Guy packs a solid punch.'

'What's he nosing around for?'

'Fudge told me that Wakefield asked him to make a fancy marker for Sandy's grave. I'd guess they are killing time until it's finished.'

'You say the young one — he went over to Crenshaw's place for supper last night?'

'That's right. I had Phelps keep an eye on him. He bought some groceries for the family and I think they were obliged to offer him hospitality.'

71

Talbot gave a nod of approval. 'And later last night, the Wakefield boys spent the night in the loft at the barn?'

'Yeah. I braced Flint at your place to check him out. He was protecting his brother when he took on Sparks. He don't seem like the sort of guy who would cause any trouble.'

'Any word on that other fellow, the one Sandy contacted?'

'I got a wire from a friend,' Bullet said. 'We'll know when he reaches Faro Junction.'

'We don't want him coming in here and asking a lot of questions.'

Bullet snorted. 'I plan to turn him around long before he gets to Orphan Creek. You can count on me, boss.'

'Any chance of the Wakefield boys learning about him?'

'No way I can think of. I took a look through Sandy's things when I boxed them up and moved them to the livery. If he was sending letters back and forth, he must have read and then burned them.'

'Keep your eyes and ears open. We don't want any surprises.'

He didn't have to say more. Bullet knew his job. 'I'll handle it, Mr Talbot.'

'Send word to Coop and Spinner. I want a mine owners' meeting this afternoon. If the death of those two old-timers or this Wakefield begins to stir things up, I want full co-operation in dealing with the situation.'

'I'll tell them what . . . right after lunch?'

'Make it two o'clock. I've an errand to run before lunch.'

Bullet didn't move for a moment. When Talbot looked at him, he was obviously waiting to speak. 'Something else?' he asked.

'One last thing concerning Shelby and Sandy,' Bullet said. 'Everyone knew they were careful miners, and they were also popular with the men. I'm thinking there are a few of the men who might suspect their deaths were not an accident. If there is trouble, you only have me and my two deputies to handle it. An uprising by a hundred miners is something we are not equipped to deal with.'

'It won't come to that.'

'I'm only saying — '

'So long as R.W. Pitkin is governor, we have all the support we need. Haw Tabor had a strike at his chrysolite mine early this summer and the governor authorized the use of a special militia to put the miners in their place. Those men who had caused the trouble were exiled from the camp and several were thrown in jail for two months each.'

'Haw Tabor is a rich man, Mr Talbot. Do you think that Pitkin would do the same for you as he did for him?'

'All it would take is a sizeable contribution to the man's campaign fund. Being a politician, he is more readily directed by money than votes.'

'Whatever you say.' Bullet ended that line of conversation. 'I'll pass the word to the other two mine owners about your meeting.'

'Good,' Talbot said. 'And keep an eye on our two friends. I want to know their every move.'

Bullet left the room and Talbot stood looking out his office window. He didn't like the idea of having anyone snooping around his mine. Nevertheless, to refuse access to the Wakefield boys would be the same as admitting that there was something suspicious about the death of the two miners. He had to play his cards close to the vest and maintain an impassive face. In a poker game of life and death, the first man to flinch was most often the first to die.

* * *

The man in charge of the working shift called himself Swede. He explained that the moniker was simpler than trying to teach people the correct pronunciation of his given name. He escorted Flint and Johnny into the mine a short way, then called out to a dark-skinned man.

Flint recognized Pepper Jones at once.

'The boys here vant to see where was killed their uncle, Sandy Vakefield. You will take them there?

'Shore 'nuff, Swede,' Pepper answered. 'I'll give them a quick tour.'

'*Gut, gut.*' Swede replied. 'Don' be taking too long.'

Although there were lamps all along the tunnel, Pepper picked up a carry-along lamp and turned the wick up all the way. As he started off, he held the light here and there while giving the Wakefield boys a quick overview of the mine.

'Got about a dozen stopes and chambers on this level,' he began. 'You can see that there is still some outcrop and iron hat along this first part. As we go deeper, you'll see a more pure form of quartz, some pyrite and colour from iron, copper and sulphur. The gangue is the worthless minerals that are mixed in with the ore.

'We use mules to pull up slag carts loaded with ore.' He pointed to a collection point. 'The miners on this level haul their loads to that hoisting compartment. Others in lower shafts use a cage and have the ore lifted to this main tunnel.'

The tour took them to a ladder, which Pepper explained was for an emergency exit, in case of fire or an unexpected explosion. As they ventured down several hundred feet, the heat and dust increased.

'This way,' Pepper said, going down a narrow tunnel. 'There are a dozen winzes along here — passages that connect to the main tunnel. Sandy and Shelby were off working in a stope — that's what we call it when we have to use step-shaped digging — at the end of this here corridor.'

Flint spied several miners down different passages, all without shirts. Their pale bodies were muscular, streaked with dirt and glistened in the dim light from beads of sweat. The lighting was remarkably good from the different candles and lamps, but everywhere remained lingering dust and nauseating fumes that burned a man's eyes and lungs. Not yet in the mine for fifteen minutes, Flint could taste grit in his mouth and feel the build up of powder along his teeth.

'Doesn't seem to be much support on some of those side tunnels,' Johnny pointed out.

'If a man don't average a fathom a day — that is six feet of digging by measure or weight — they don't get full wages. There's a guy called Weasel who checks each and every miner at the end of his shift.'

'Weasel?'

'He was recruited by Talbot to oversee the miners' daily progress. His real name is Ormund Wessinger, but the nickname fits and he doesn't seem to mind. He is happy to be doing the audits rather than working the mine.'

'The inside of this mountain certainly looks like a tough go,' Johnny spoke up.

Pepper laughed without mirth. 'Yeah, in this kind of rock, it's a real chore to make enough progress to get full pay. Shoring up takes time and don't earn a man a cent. We get by with as little as possible.'

'Wouldn't extra timber maybe prevent a cave-in?' Flint asked. 'Seems the mine owners would be in favour of that much additional safety.'

'There ain't no shortage of miners, Flint,' Pepper replied. 'If one of us is crippled or killed, there are a dozen waiting in line to step into our job.'

'That would make me feel real secure,' Johnny quipped.

They reached the dark end of the passage and Pepper stopped. He motioned to a pile of rubble. 'This is it. Didn't have much colour here, but them two old-timers figured to hit a streak in the next few feet. They were real smart about where to dig.'

Flint took the lantern from Pepper and ventured forward. The debris was still piled to either side of the cave opening, where rock and dirt had been thrown aside. There was no hint of timbering, so the miners must have thought the rocky surface did not yet need support.

Inching into the cramped chamber, Flint held the lantern high. 'Where did the explosion come from?'

Pepper edged in behind him and pointed. 'Appears they had it set high up on the left side — somewhere about here. You can see the crater from the blast.'

Flint stood and stared at the spot. Then he went the last few feet into the small recess and carefully explored the wall on all sides. He stopped, when he stepped on a drill bit. A double-jack hammer was only inches away. Hunkering down, he dug out a couple of bits from the dirt.

'That short one is the starter drill. We call it the bull steel. Each of the others is for widening the hole and going in deeper. Got to be about thirty inches deep before you can set the dynamite.'

'Anyone been in here to inspect the site?'

'Not as far as I know,' Pepper replied. 'Ain't no one been assigned to continue the dig down this way yet.'

Scrutinizing the surrounding walls, Flint discerned a bore hole in the face of the rock. A careful review about produced a second hole. 'Looks like they were working to set a charge to the front, Pepper. Would they blast from two directions at the same time?'

Pepper came over and wiped the dust from around the hole. He took measure of the surrounding area and looked back to where they were standing. A shock realization entered his expression.

'You're right about that, Flint. We usually set a blast pattern of five to seven holes in the direction of the dig. A good blast will remove about three feet of rock. I sure don't see any reason they would have for setting a charge to the rear of where they were digging.' Studying the rock walls, he added, 'Besides that, there ain't any colour trace: the ceiling was high enough; can't see no reason for blasting there in the roof at all. We thought the accident happened when they were widening the chamber, so no one bothered to look for any other holes. You can see that these holes up front are aligned along the colour line, where they were digging out and blasting to hopefully find higher grade ore.'

'What's your gut tell you, Pepper?' Johnny asked. 'You are the one with experience in mining. Was this an accident or not?'

The man's face was drawn tight, his jaw anchored in place. He stuck the drill bit into the hole and shoved it in as far as it would go. When he removed it, his eyes flicked about nervously, as if he feared someone might be listening.

'This don't look good,' he whispered. 'If Sandy and Todd were busy drilling this hole, then someone else must have set off the dynamite behind them!'

'And that would make this a murder, not a mining accident.'

Pepper shook his head, as if unable to

believe the words. 'But why would anyone want to kill them two fellows? They was liked by everyone.'

'Could have been someone trying to kill just one of them,' Johnny suggested. 'You know of any enemies of either Shelby or our uncle?'

'Nary a one,' Pepper replied.

'There must be an explanation.'

'I'd sure like to hear it,' Pepper said. 'The hole for the blast would have had to be an old drill hole, or one that was put there when no one was working in the mine. If someone wanted to kill Sandy and Todd, they only had to slip in behind them and light the dynamite. When a hammer is banging on a drill, you're half blind with dust and your ears are ringing too much to notice anything as faint as a fuse burning.'

'We're still talking a big if,' Johnny said. 'We don't know for sure that the two men weren't enlarging the chamber. Maybe they wanted more room to work.'

'I don't think so, not by the location of the hole they were drilling,' Pepper pointed out. 'They had nothing to gain by blowing rock from the roof section. As I said, there ain't any sign of colour, no advantage to taking out that rock at all.'

'Keep this knowledge to yourself, Pepper,' Flint warned. 'We're going to do a little snooping around on our own and we wouldn't want any accidents happening to you.'

'You don't have to tell me twice,' he said in a hushed voice. 'You boys seen enough?'

'Let's get out of here,' Johnny was first to reply. 'I prefer the open air and sunshine. This being cooped up underground is not for me.'

'A toplander like Fudge,' Pepper remarked. 'I often think that's where I belong too.'

Flint went along in silence while his mind was turning over a number of actions and possibilities. He was not an investigator, but he was reasonably certain a crime had been committed.

So what now? he asked himself. How

do I proceed? Who do I turn to for help? And if someone did cause the death of Sandy and Shelby, is it possible they will try and silence Johnny and me, too?

4

As Lavera walked slowly toward the company store, she searched through her memory for a miracle. She was not Moses. She could not turn a handful of flour and three stale crackers into a fitting meal. The combining of the wages both she and Shawn earned might be enough to pay the rent and buy a minimum of coal to keep from freezing, but what about other necessities?

How do we eat? she wondered. What about clothing, medicine or work boots for Shawn? And I'll never be able to afford the thread and lace to even make a new dress from flour sacks!

Reaching into her pocket, she withdrew the coins she had received as tips the previous night. Sixty-four cents. If not for Sandy's nephew, she would have made almost nothing. Talbot had been right. Waiting tables would not earn sufficient funds to keep her family in food and clothing.

The fragrance inside the store caused her stomach to growl and her mouth to water. Gates's wife had removed loaves of freshly baked bread only moments earlier. The heavenly scent reminded Lavera that it had been two weeks since she had managed the ingredients for even bread. Her father had insisted they stockpile what wood and coal they could each payday, preparing for the cold winter months. How she would miss his planning and decision-making.

'Good morning, Miss Shelby,' Mr Gates greeted her. 'Can I help you with anything today?'

'No, thank you,' she replied. 'I only need a couple of items.'

'Well, Mr Talbot says the sky is the limit for you.' Gates had an insightful twinkle in his eyes and Lavera was all too aware of what he was thinking.

'That's very nice of him, but I don't intend to run up a bill.'

'Same as your father,' Gates returned cheerfully. 'It must be a family trait not to go into debt for more than a week's pay.'

'Something like that.'

'Well, you need anything at all you only have to say the word.'

Mrs Jones entered the front door and stopped to inhale the wonderful aroma. 'Lawdy!' she exclaimed, 'that fresh bread do smell good today, Mrs Gates.'

'Good morning, Selma,' Mrs Gates greeted Pepper's wife. 'You want two loaves today?'

'Yes, ma'am, I does,' Selma replied, her speech reflecting both her rich accent and her lack of education.

Lavera nodded a salutation to Selma. They had not spoken often, as the only two Negro ladies in camp usually kept pretty much to themselves. Todd had told her that Selma came from the deep south where there were very few schools. Selma seemed to be a sweet woman and she and Pepper gave the impression of being happy together.

The same could be said for Fudge and Maisy.

'I'se sorry, Miss Lavera,' Selma spoke to her quietly. 'Me and Maisy din' come to your house and extend our sorrow yesterday.'

'Think nothing of it, Mrs Jones. We had already spoken at the funeral. It wasn't necessary.'

The woman's face softened. 'Sure going to be hard on you all, not having no man in your house.'

'Shawn is nearly grown.'

She bobbed her head, but there was a real concern in her eyes. 'I'se don' know what would happen if my Pepper was kilt that way. I'se got a new child comin' — she patted her slightly protruding tummy to accentuate the fact she was several months pregnant — 'and sure wouldn't want tuh raise this young 'un all by myself.'

'A death is always much harder on those miners with family,' Lavera agreed.

'I'se done got me a look at them two

boys, the ones that come fo' Mister Wakefield's funeral,' Selma changed the subject. 'Good-lookin' gents, them two.'

'Mr Wakefield's nephews,' Lavera concluded.

'Yes, my Pepper done told me.' She smiled. 'He say Flint Wakefield be a nice man.'

'I met him last night.'

Mr Gates set two loaves of bread on the counter for Selma. 'Will that be all for you, Mrs Jones?'

'One more loaf,' she said, 'fo' Miss Lavera. I meant tuh bring somethin' by your house yesterday.'

'Oh! You don't have to do that, Mrs Jones. Really!'

But Selma smiled. 'Take it, child. It don' be charity, it be fo' missing the visit yesterday.'

'Thank you, Mrs Jones. You really shouldn't, but thank you.'

Selma picked up the other two loaves of bread. 'You write me down fo' three?' she asked Gates.

The storekeeper had a ledger in his

hand. He turned it around to show Selma. 'Right there.' He pointed to the column. 'See? Three for today.'

'Tha's fine,' she said. 'I be back on Monday fo' two more.'

'Good day to you, Mrs Jones.'

Lavera picked out six eggs, removing them from the lime-water and placing them on the counter. She carefully counted out sixty cents and handed it to the storekeeper.

'While there are no other customers in the store, Lavera, I should bring you up to date on your account,' Gates said, turning the ledger around so she could see the figures. 'This page is the one for your family.' He pointed to the name at the top of the sheet. 'You can see the balance and dates.' He continued to explain his bookkeeping. 'When the cave-in took your pa, he owed twenty-three dollars and some change. However, he had two days' pay coming for this past week and the mine owners put up twenty-five dollars as a death benefit. That leaves you with a credit of almost eight dollars. I can either give you cash for that amount, or you can leave it on your account and use it as you wish here at the store.'

Lavera had forgotten the mine owners usually donated a little something to widows and orphans. Eight dollars was not a fortune, but she decided to spend some of it immediately.

'Now that you mention it, I think I will pick up a couple more items. Maybe I'll fix the boys something special today.'

'We got a shipment of pork and some fryers this week,' Gates suggested. 'Either one would make a fine Sunday dinner.'

A sudden thought came to Lavera. 'Chicken, I think. I'd like one of those fryers.'

★　★　★

Johnny hunkered over the camp-fire, stirring the beans. 'This isn't exactly what I had in mind for breakfast, Flint,' he grumbled. 'I could have gotten us an invite at the Crenshaw place.'

Flint looked up the canyon, toward the secluded mining town. Up at sun-up, they had ridden a short way to a small stream, where there was adequate kindling for a fire. He reached down and removed the percolating pot of coffee from next to the fire, poured some into a cup and sighed.

'You said the woman of the house was down sick and her husband is nursing a broken foot.'

'Yeah, but her daughter is a pretty good cook.' Johnny winked. 'She's cute as a month-old puppy too.'

'It's not enough that she is doing laundry to earn a few cents a day, you want her to tend to a sick family, look after her younger brothers and sisters, and then take time to prepare meals for a couple strangers? You've got a big heart, little brother.'

'I spent over six dollars on food for them,' he objected. 'It isn't exactly mooching to accept a meal or two in return.'

'Charity isn't supposed to have strings attached,' Flint told him. 'Besides, you stayed and had supper with them last night.'

Johnny grinned. 'Yeah, and I'll bet Meg's cooking was a whole lot better than what you got at the tavern.'

'You noticed we didn't go there for breakfast,' Flint replied. 'The steak I had was as tough as sunparched boot leather.'

Johnny's smile faded and he grew serious. 'I don't know what those people are going to do, Flint. Al Crenshaw's foot needs another month to heal properly. He told me that he was going back to work next week, but he can't even put weight on the foot yet.'

'I noticed more than a few men with long faces myself. And the price of food at the company store is pretty steep.'

'I checked on the price of coal for their stoves — two-bits a sack and it lasts about two days, even less in the cold months. Add in oil for their lamps — even the ingredients for candles are expensive — and that's for stuff like mutton tallow, camphor, beeswax and alum. A person ought to be able to make candles for about two-bits a hundred. I'll bet that buying the makings at the company store, it costs darn near a cent per candle. When you study on it, these people are not much better off than indentured convicts.'

'That's what they are, Johnny, slaves to the job. The mine owners offer three dollars a day for working a ten-hour shift in their mines. On the face of it, it sounds like big money and draws in unsuspecting workers who think they can earn a good living. Then they find out the company housing is twenty dollars a month and it takes another fifteen dollars for heat and cooking fuel. Combine that with the price for food, clothes and tools which are triple what they had thought. I'll bet most of these men end up deeper in debt every month and have no way to get out.'

'That young Davy is working seven days a week tending mules. Al told me that there are other children working clean-up and dumping or moving slag. Some of those kids have ended up with broken bones and a couple have died in accidents.'

'I don't know what we can do about it, Johnny. The mine owners aren't doing anything illegal. In fact, it's the same all over the country, no matter what kind of ore is being mined. You remember hearing about the Molly Maguires? They tried to break the steel grip of the anthracite coalfield mine owners. After endless months of terror and killing, nothing really changed, except for twenty of those men involved — they were hanged.'

'I know, but . . . '

'And think back to this past summer,' said Flint, not allowing his brother's protest, 'Governor Pitkin sent guns and ammunition to Tabor's hired troops to squash the miner's strike in Leadville. The mine owners have the money and it gives them the power to do as they please.'

'But it isn't right, Flint!'

'I don't think right has a thing to do with it.'

Johnny removed the pan from the fire. 'The beans are ready.'

The two of them ate in relative silence. Once finished, Flint rinsed the pan off in the stream. They shared a second cup of coffee, each mulling over his own thoughts.

'You're studying law, Flint,' Johnny said at length. 'Isn't there something in the books that says you have to sell merchandise at a decent price?'

'Whatever the market will bear, I'm afraid. In some of the mining towns, back where access is nearly impossible, prices are inflated a hundred times over. I remember when I was a little kid how a friend of Dad's hired a couple of men to drive a small herd of beef back into the mining camps. He sold those cattle for two and three hundred dollars apiece — made himself a fortune.'

'Yeah, but that's for people who made the choice themselves. These miners are getting a short-loop. There's a train that comes to within twenty miles of this place. The shipping charges from there can't be high enough to justify the prices at the company store.'

'That's true enough, but the miners can't take two or three days off to travel to the next town for the single purpose of buying supplies. Besides which, a good many mines pay in scrip or keep account records instead of making actual payments to the miners. They don't have ready cash in hand to go spend elsewhere.'

Johnny flipped his wrist, emptying the grounds from his cup. 'It leaves a bad taste in your mouth,' showing a grim expression, 'worse even than this here coffee.'

'I agree.'

As the younger Wakefield rinsed his cup at the stream, Flint considered the situation. There were always options open, alternatives to any given circumstance. He knew Sandy was an intelligent guy and he had worked at other mines. It made him wonder if he had been of a mind to do something to make life better for the miners at Orphan Creek. If so, it might present a motive for why he and Shelby were killed.

'What now?' Johnny asked.

'I've got a meeting with Miss Shelby at noon. I'll see if she has any information to add or has any ideas of her own about the accident.'

'What about me?'

'Did you talk to Crenshaw about the possibility of Sandy's death not being a mishap, or were you too busy ogling Meg?'

'I'll slip over there about lunchtime too,' he evaded. 'Might even pick up some bread or rolls from the store first.'

'All right. Fudge said he would have the headstone finished on Monday. We'll be around another couple days yet.'

'After the marker is placed, we head for home?' Johnny asked. 'We forget about Uncle Sandy maybe being murdered and the rotten deal these miners have up here?'

'We'll see what else we can learn first,' Flint replied. 'I'll send a wire to Pa and tell him about the headstone and our delay so he doesn't worry about us.'

'Good thinking, big brother.' Johnny grinned, 'After all, you're the one Pa will hold responsible.'

★ ★ ★

Lavera opened the door, expecting to see Flint, Sandy Wakefield's nephew. She was both surprised and dismayed to discover the visitor was Henry Talbot. He was dressed in an expensive brown suit, complete with string tie and polished boots. He removed the fashionable straw hat in a gentlemanly gesture. It revealed his black, wavy hair, except for traces of grey at the temples. He was not altogether unattractive for his age which she guessed to be near or into his early forties. He smiled a greeting.

'Miss Shelby, good day to you.'

She narrowed her gaze. 'What are you doing here, Mr Talbot?'

'I wanted to check and see how you were,' he replied smoothly. 'Is there anything that you need?'

She bit back a cynical reply about knowing what he really wanted and managed to remain civil. 'Why the deep concern?'

A hurtful expression came into his face. 'My dear Lavera, I am always concerned that my employees are happy. I watched you work tables for a time last night — very impressive. Cracker told me that you tended to more tables than the other two girls combined.'

'That shouldn't be any wonder. They spent much of their time sitting with the customers. I told you I don't — '

'Yes, I know,' he interrupted her and gave a dismissive wave of his hand, 'you don't intend to drink with the customers.'

'That's right.'

'It will be busier tonight, being that it's Friday,' he warned. 'And Saturday is even worse. I fear you will wear yourself out if you don't sit down once in a while.'

She ignored the suggestion she sit with some of the miners and asked, 'Did you have a purpose in coming here today?'

'I wanted you to know that I have authorized you to charge whatever you like at the store. If you should need anything — '

'That's very nice of you,' it was her turn to cut him short, 'but I don't intend to run our account up so high that I can't possibly pay for it.'

Talbot studied her for a moment. The earthy repose was unsettling, but Lavera held her ground. His unveiled scrutiny caused her to feel like a horse up for auction, being inspected before the sale.

Talbot sighed, while toying with his hat, rotating it in his hands. 'It's a lonely world up here, Lavera, even for a man like me. I tried to tell you as much at your job interview.'

She held her breath, unable to summon words.

'Now, after watching you work so diligently at the tavern, it occurred to me that you might be lonely too. I don't recall ever seeing you socializing with, or being escorted by, any of the miners.'

'I don't wish to be courted by a miner,' she answered him candidly.

'Really?'

'There is no future in it. My father was a very careful man, yet he is dead. I've listened to the men cough at nights from breathing in the stale, dirty air, seen the red in their eyes from the dusty grit and observed the smashed bones and daily scrapes and bruises. I don't intend to sit at home and worry each day that my husband will not return to me a whole man.'

'I understand your feelings,' Talbot said. 'Really, I do.'

Lavera looked over her shoulder. 'I have food cooking on the stove, Mr

Talbot. I'm sorry, but I don't have time to stand here and chat.'

'Perhaps we could talk another time.' At her hesitation, he added, 'I promise, it won't be anything which might be constructed as courting.'

She didn't wish to give him an ounce of encouragement, but he was her boss. 'I suppose, when I have nothing else to do.'

He smiled and replaced his hat. 'I'll look forward to it. What about Sunday?' he asked, displaying a shrewd and somewhat masked expression. 'Would you allow me to accompany you to the weekly prayer meeting?'

Lavera hesitated. His move was calculated to work his way into her life. She hated to allow him that foothold. It was wrong to give a man any encouragement, unless there was a mutual attraction. He was a powerful man, a man with money and influence . . . and he had given her a job.

'It's only the Sunday meeting,' he coaxed her. 'No one will give it a second thought.'

'If you like,' she finally capitulated. 'But only with the understanding that my brothers are going with us too.'

The vow brought forth a chuckle. 'Yes, yes, Lavera. It will be very forthright and proper. I would not presume to compromise your reputation.'

She didn't appreciate the way he spoke the words, as if teasing her for being chaste. However, she used his acceptance as a culmination to their conversation.

'Until Sunday morning then,' she said, stepping back into her cabin. Talbot nodded, backing away and replacing his hat. 'Good day,' he returned cordially, and she shut the door.

★ ★ ★

Bullet Skinner and Digger Phelps stepped out into the trail, blocking the way for the single rider. The man's suit and wide-brimmed hat were coated with dust from the trail. He had been hunched over in the saddle, obviously fatigued from long hours of travel.

'Good day, gentlemen,' he greeted, stopping his horse. He took notice of the badges on the vests of the two men. 'What's going on?'

'You appear headed for Orphan Creek, friend,' Bullet said. 'That right?'

'As a matter of fact, I am.'

'There is some news of a smallpox epidemic spreading about in some parts of the country. We are checking anyone coming into town.'

'Smallpox?' The man's eyebrows lifted in surprise. 'I haven't heard a thing about it.'

'Where you from?'

The man appeared to hesitate. 'I came in from Utah. There's no smallpox back the way I came.'

'Utah, you say,' Phelps spoke up. 'What are you doing in this neck of the woods?'

'Came to see some old friends.'

'Their names wouldn't be Sandy Wakefield or Todd Shelby?' Bullet challenged. 'Them two boys had an accident a couple days back — both were killed in a cave-in.'

Alarm spread across the man's face. He attempted to cover up his reaction by reaching down to pat the neck of his horse. 'I don't believe I ever met either of them,' he said, slipping his hand back to remain near his hip. 'Actually, I was going to visit with Henry Talbot.'

Bullet could see the bulge of a gun beneath his coat. He already had his own hand resting on the butt of his Colt.

'You're lying through your teeth, mister,' Phelps accused loudly. 'Wakefield and Shelby sent for you. We've been watching for you to show up for a week. I'd say our waiting is over.'

'You got me wrong,' the man said, but his face drained of colour. 'I don't want any trouble.'

'This guy they sent for walks with a limp,' Bullet said. 'You wouldn't mind getting down and taking a few steps for us?'

'What kind of nonsense is this?' the man on horseback wanted to know. 'If there is a problem concerning my visit, I'll just turn around and go back the way I came. I don't have to put up with this kind of harassment.'

'You ain't going nowhere, mister,' Phelps retorted. 'Get off'n that horse before we start throwing lead!'

The words pushed the man to panic. He clawed at his holster, attempting to draw his pistol —

Bullet jerked his own gun and fired.

Phelps pulled the trigger of his gun at nearly the same time. The man on horseback had no chance. He was unable to even get his own gun free before being hit twice in the chest. The horse, spooked by the sudden gunfire, reared up and dumped the rider onto the hard ground.

Bullet watched the horse bolt back down the winding trail until it was lost from sight. He and Phelps walked over to check on their kill. Bending over the man, he went through the papers in his pocket and grunted his satisfaction.

'This is the guy we were looking for,' he remarked to Phelps. 'Ain't no doubt he's the one Shelby and Wakefield sent for.'

'What'll we do with him?'

'Strip him down and toss him into the ravine. We'll feed him to the ants and coyotes.'

As Phelps began to undress the body, Bullet walked a few paces down the trail. He hated to have the horse running loose, but no telling how far the mangy critter would run. It wasn't worth trying to chase him down. Even if someone saw the horse, there was little chance they would track down the body. It was probable that the animal had been rented at Faro Junction, in which case it would return to its stable. Even if a search party was sent out because of the riderless horse, and even if they somehow managed to find the body, there was nothing to connect the murder with the mines at Orphan Creek. By stripping the body, it would appear to be a robbery.

Phelps dragged the body off the trail and sent it rolling down a steep bank. As he returned, he showed a cocky grin and said, 'That takes care of that.'

Bullet nodded in agreement, wondering how a man could kill another human being and apparently have no conscience or remorse at all. He had been following orders, doing his job. He regretted having to resort to murder. Phelps, however, had come along for the *fun* of it. He was as cold-blooded as a snake.

'What about the nag?' Phelps asked.

'It'll be halfway back down to Faro Junction by this time. I didn't see any saddle-bags or blanket roll on him. Our dead friend must have left his belongings down at the junction — probably the boarding-house. If his rented horse returns without him, they might send someone out to look for him, but there ain't much chance of finding his body in that ravine.'

'So we head back to town?'

'Yeah, we did the job that had to be done. We can report back to Talbot that he doesn't have to worry about that nosy jack showing up now.'

'What about the guy's clothes and stuff?'

'Burn everything — clothes, papers, shoes, the works.'

'You got it, boss. There won't be nothing left except a pile of ashes when I get finished. You can count on it.'

Bullet watched the man stuff the clothes and few belongings into a sack. It wasn't much of an epitaph for a man's life.

5

The door opened to the wonderfully enticing aroma of fried chicken. Lavera was wearing a pink, plain cotton dress, with a flour-sack apron around her waist. The dress was obviously aged, frayed a bit about the collar and hem, but freshly laundered and snug enough to accent the young lady's nubile form. Lavera put a hand up to brush a strand of stray hair back from her face.

'I was starting to think that you had forgotten about coming to see me,' she said, displaying a smile of greeting which caused Flint's heart to flutter about like a moth in a jar.

'No, ma'am.' He found both his voice and aplomb. 'I figured you might be sleeping late, what with you having to work till after midnight.'

'Would you care to join us for dinner?' she offered. 'I was about to set the table. Shawn will be coming home for lunch pretty soon.'

'I'd be honoured, Miss Shelby. A person would not be likely to grow fat eating at your place of employment.'

'I cleared your table,' she said, flashing a knowing smile. 'When the cook threw out the left-over steak, I saw two dogs fighting over which one *had* to eat it.'

He laughed at her humour and entered the small cabin. 'You sure I'm not imposing?'

'Not at all.'

'Well, I don't think I've ever smelled anything with a more delicious aroma than the chicken you're frying. I'll forever be in your debt.'

She smiled at his remark, her eyes twinkling with something that resembled satisfaction. He experienced an immediate warmth at the thought she might have planned the meal especially for his benefit.

A boy of about ten or eleven appeared from out of the shadows. He looked Flint over from head to toe, finally focusing his attention on his .44-40 Frontier Colt.

'You a gunfighter?' he asked, his eyes wide with wonder.

'I've come into contact with thieves, rustlers, bandits and murderers, young fella, but never a gunfighter. There are a few hired killers, but an actual gunfighter is mostly a fabrication of Eastern writers.'

'Do that mean there ain't none?'

'Aren't any!' Lavera correct his grammar. 'How many times have I told you not to use *ain't*, Grant?'

''Least a million,' he sighed.

'Go fetch your brother for dinner. I'm not going to let this chicken burn waiting for him.'

'All right, Vera, I'm going.'

As Grant went out the door, Flint took a moment to survey the interior of the two-room, wooden shack. Beneath the plate settings for four, there was a well-worn tablecloth spread over a crude sawbuck table. About the table were four peg-leg stools. Along one wall was a work counter with cupboards above and below, a dishpan, and a small cast-iron stove that served for both heat and cooking. Also within the main room, there was a cot, undoubtedly utilized for both sitting as well as one of the necessary beds. In the adjacent room, he could see bunk beds — the boys' sleeping quarters. A closet was also visible, with one other dress and two black suit coats. The wooden walls of the shanty were not completely weatherproof. Although covered with pasteboard, he could see slivers of daylight though a number of cracks. He could imagine the howling winter wind seeping through between the boards to freeze the occupants inside.

'There's a wash pan if you need to rinse off the dust,' Lavera offered, tilting her head slightly to indicate a simple washing stand and neatly folded cloth for a towel.

'I did my morning scrub and shave at the creek outside of town,' Flint informed her. 'Nothing like an icy stream to freshen up your day.'

'So, where are you from, Mr Wakefield?' Lavera asked, turning her back to him. He moved over behind the girl and watched her work. She was using a fork to turn the pieces of chicken and he suspected she was keenly aware of his presence.

'We've a small ranch outside of Colorado Springs. My father is a retired judge.'

'And what do you do, ride herd on the cattle?'

'Some,' he said, 'but for the past coupla years I've been studying to become a lawyer.'

She rotated her head enough to look over her shoulder at him. 'Yes, I can picture you as a lawyer.'

'I've got another year or so to go before I can go before a board and get certified.'

She let out a sigh. 'I wish my brothers had a chance to do something with their lives. There certainly isn't any future here. Working the mines is hard, it's dangerous and it destroys the body. Dad once told me your uncle was the oldest miner he had ever met.'

'Speaking of the mines, I visited the Excalibur and looked over the explosion site yesterday. I have to tell you, Miss Shelby, I'm not at all certain the blast that killed your father and my uncle was an accident.'

His statement drew an immediate stare, eyes sharp enough to force him back a step. 'What do you mean?' she asked. 'What have you learned about the cave-in?'

'From the point where the explosive went off, it appears the blast came from both above and behind them,' he explained. 'Pepper Jones was there with my brother and me at the location of the accident and, after a thorough examination of the scene, we concluded there was no practical reason for the two of them to be setting a charge in the cave ceiling.'

Lavera's lips formed a tight line. 'So

you believe they were murdered?'

'It appears as if someone wanted to be rid of either Sandy or your father. Can you think of any reason why someone would want to kill either of them?'

Lavera took a moment to test the creamed potatoes. When she met Flint's gaze, there were tears in her eyes.

'I can't imagine anyone wanting to hurt my father or your uncle, Mr Wakefield. They were liked by everyone.'

'There might be another reason,' he suggested gently. 'Were either of them on any kind of committee, a jury at a kangaroo court, maybe involved in anything where two sides were in disagreement?'

She thought a moment and said, 'The only thing I can think of is they were both on a safety committee, but it was a title without position or authority. They would help train a new miner, or suggest to the owners how something could be done easier, or with less risk.

They were responsible for adding more lighting in the tunnels and making it mandatory to clear the men from all levels from a blasting zone, that sort of thing. If they ever had a major argument with someone about something to do with the mines, Father never said a word about it.'

'No problems with the mine owners that you know of?'

'The safety rules they implemented saved injuries and in turn kept more men on the job. They always took their suggestions to the mine owners for approval before it was put into use. Some of their ideas became policy at all three mines.'

'What about the living conditions here?' Flint changed directions. 'The high prices at the store and paying rent must keep everyone broke.'

'We don't have any control over those things. I remember Father complaining to Mr Gates one time, but he said the prices were set by Mr Talbot. He's the one who actually owns the store.'

'They still work ten-hour days here. I read recently where some mines have cut their days to eight-hour shifts. Any possibility that they were working on something like that?'

'They used to talk about it, of course, but the mine owners said it would cost too much money. They allowed the miners could go to eight-hour shifts, but only if they took a cut in wages. No one could afford that.'

The door opened, preventing him from asking any further questions. Shawn was already rolling up his sleeves, heading for the wash basin. Grant was right on his heels.

'Sis,' Shawn sounded off, 'I could smell that chicken all the way up to the mine! I don't remember when we had it last.'

'I do,' Grant spoke up. 'It was for Christmas dinner.'

'You wash your hands too, Grant,' Lavera told the younger boy sternly. 'And both of you try and show some manners at the table. We have a guest for dinner.'

Shawn dried off with a towel and came over to shake Flint's hand. He displayed a natural grin and a firm grip.

'I heard about you feeding Sparks a mouthful of knuckles yesterday,' he said. 'Wish I'd have been there to see it.'

'Wasn't all that much to see,' Flint answered, noticing a curious frown of disapproval on Lavera's face. 'Johnny, my younger brother, was the one who got into the fracas. I only stopped Sparks from teaching him a lesson.' He attempted a grin. 'Maybe I made a mistake there. A good beating might be what he needs to keep from getting into fixes like that.'

'I know what you mean,' Shawn affirmed. 'I'm always having to watch over Grant to keep him out of trouble.'

'Do not!' Grant cried.

'Do so,' Shawn shot back.

'Not!'

'Let it drop, boys!' Lavera told them

both. 'I told you to behave. If you wish to leave without eating, keep right on arguing.'

'Who's arguing?' Shawn asked with complete innocence.

'Yeah, we're best friends — like brothers!' Grant joined in, displaying a wide grin and putting his arm around Shawn. 'We was only funning.'

'Sit down,' she ordered. 'You too, Mr Wakefield.'

He exhibited a disarming smile. 'Whatever you say, Miss Shelby.'

'And you may as well call me Lavera — everyone else does.'

'I'll consider that an honour . . . Lavera.'

The young lady blushed noticeably, something the two boys observed, but both were intelligent enough not to mention. Flint had to ponder her embarrassment, curious as to how many men had been treated to one of Lavera's invites for dinner.

The meal was as good as it had smelled. Flint kept a tight rein on his appetite, taking heed of the fact that the boys were prone to gnawing their meat until the bone was whisker clean. From the fairly gaunt faces in the room, he guessed they did not eat hearty meals very often. When Shawn had finished his meal he said a quick goodbye and was back off to work.

Lavera rose from the table and Flint immediately stood up, too. His gentlemanly act caused her a momentary uncertainty.

'Grant,' she said, recovering quickly, 'the chore of cleaning up belongs to you. I don't want to find the dishes covered with grease.'

'Yeah, Vera,' he said glumly.

'And save the chicken bones for soup.'

'Yeah, Vera, I'll do a good job.'

'Thank you, Grant,' she said. Then, turning to Flint, 'Mr Wakefield, perhaps we could take a short walk.'

'If you are allowing me the privilege of calling you by your first name, then it's only appropriate that you address me by mine — I go by Flint.'

She hesitated for a brief moment, as if she would argue the point. Then she gave a slight nod. 'Very well, Flint.'

He walked ahead of her and opened the door. As she passed though, he detected a slight rise in her natural colour. He wondered again how many suitors Lavera had entertained before and decided it could not have been many.

Keeping pace with the girl, Flint allowed her to choose their path. She led him beyond the rows of houses, until they reached the face of the mountain. They manoeuvred between a stand of brush and several trees, following a faint trail that skirted the side of the mountain. Finally, Lavera stopped at a smooth-faced stone wall. Near the base was a large clearing, one that commanded a view of the valley below. From such a lofty perch, the rise of cliffs and canyon floors were lost to the panoramic maze of pine and fur trees which covered the higher mountains.

'I often come here to read or be alone,' she said, moving over to sit down on a large slab of flat rock. 'As you can see, it's one of the most beautiful views imaginable. And even in the winter, this rock catches the heat from the sun.'

Impulsively, he thought of her lying out to bask in the sun, a human cat, stretching lazily, soaking up the heat rays. He was struck by the inviting impression of a playful sprite or impish wood nymph.

'What are you smiling at?' She caught his expression.

'Just thinking,' he replied.

'I wonder that I can trust being alone with you,' she said, her brows drawing together suspiciously. 'I don't even know what kind of man you are.'

'The kind that would never take advantage of a young lady,' he was quick to respond. 'My mother is a very proper woman. Ever since I was knee high to a Colorado grasshopper, she demanded I show the utmost respect for womanhood.'

Lavera studied him for a moment. 'Womanhood,' she repeated. 'That's an odd term.'

'She told me I should treat every woman as if she were my best friend's mother. It made no difference if the woman was a street harlot or the neighbourhood witch. I was taught to grant them proper regard until they proved to me personally that they didn't deserve it.'

'How many Wakefields are there?'

'Boyd, Sandy, Carlyle and Trudy all came from England with my grandfather back in the '50s. After the War Between the States, the family broke up. Carlyle and Trudy went further West, while Boyd took up ranching here in Colorado. Sandy never did put down roots, but he came by to visit once or twice each year. Carlyle married a Mormon woman and joined their church for a time. He has five kids and ended up down in California. Trudy met and married a banker in Nevada.

She has two boys and a girl.'

'You're part of a large family.'

'I suppose.'

'And is Johnny your only brother?'

'No, there's Doherty, whom we've called Doc since he was a kid. He was always trying to mend a scratch on a calf's leg or fix a bird's busted wing. He's at medical school right now, so I guess his nickname will come to pass for real. I also have a younger sister back home.'

'I had an uncle,' Lavera said. 'He was killed in the war. My mother died of fever back a few years when Grant was still a baby.'

'You've been dealt a tough hand. Being the eldest in the family, I figure you now feel responsible for both of your brothers.'

'We got by while my father was alive. Now that he's gone, however, it's going to be difficult to make ends meet.'

'Especially with the prices around here.'

'The mine owners claim the expense

of shipping is why everything up here cost so much.'

'I suppose that could be true, but it's only about twenty miles down to Faro Junction. The narrow gauge railroad being used for hauling ore goes that far. The supplies could be shipped back on it, meaning things should be a little less expensive than having it brought here by wagon. With the Denver and South Park Railroad going right through Faro Junction, I should think they could order and have goods shipped from Denver at a reasonable rate.'

A light of interest entered her eyes. 'My father used to speak the same way. He was one of the few who dared to speak out about how we were being robbed at the company store.'

'Is that so?'

'I remember him saying a while back that the miners should form a union. He said, if everyone would work together, they could force the mine owners to offer either higher wages or lower prices for coal and food.'

'Did he do anything about organizing the miners?'

'Not that I know of. I always assumed it was just so much talk.'

'Uncle Sandy worked at the Comstock mine over in Nevada for a few months a couple of years back. He told us about the union miners there. He said that they worked eight-hour days, at three dollars fifty per day, plus the mine kept medical help available for the miners. I recall him saying something about the problems in Leadville and some of these other mines the last time he came to visit.'

Flint discovered that Lavera was staring at him. He was temporarily mesmerized. He could read the question within the depths of her shimmering, aquamarine eyes.

'You don't think that — ' she whispered, her lips barely mouthing the words.

'I don't want to jump to any conclusions,' he forced his voice to respond.

'They wouldn't kill Sandy and my

father for mere talk about a union!'

'I really don't know, Lavera. I'm going to do some checking while we're waiting on the headstone for Sandy. There is still a remote possibility the explosion could have been an accident.'

'But you don't believe that — I can see you don't.'

'What I suspect is not the issue here. If I have learned anything of law, it's that the only real crimes are the ones you can prove in a court before a judge and jury. Suspicions alone do not bring about justice.'

'So you will be staying here in Orphan Creek, while you do your checking around?'

'Probably, though I really haven't decided on the best way to proceed yet.'

'I really hate the idea that my father and Sandy might have been murdered. It was hard enough to accept their deaths as an accident.'

'If there was foul play behind their deaths, we have to find evidence to prove it. I haven't yet figured out the best way to proceed.'

'You won't proceed very far if someone decides to kill you.'

Flint displayed a cocky smile. 'I'm not going into the mines a second time. If they decide to cut me out of the picture, I'll at least have a chance to see them coming.'

'You appear to be a man of honour,' Lavera said, gently placing her hand over his own. 'I hope you'll be careful.'

'Like a mongoose playing with a cobra,' he quipped.

'I wonder how many mongoose have lost when playing that game of death.'

'Not to worry, fair lady, I have my brother with me. If trouble comes it will find him first . . . it always does.'

She smiled. 'Like at the store?'

Flint chuckled. 'I swear that kid has an internal magnet which attracts any kind of mischief around.'

'It was admirable, him sticking up for Davy Crenshaw.'

'It was trouble and he was drawn in like a bee to a flower blossom.'

131

'You are the more mature, yet you were the one who ended up doing the fighting.'

'Johnny has a habit of handing off his troubles to me.'

'Well, you will have to be careful all the same. If someone did kill Father and your uncle, they won't hesitate to kill you too.'

Flint was touched at her genuine sentiment. He studied her for a long moment before speaking, enchanted by her inner radiance. It appeared she had a world of beauty hidden beneath the surface and only allowed a tiny portion to shine through.

'A man called Byron wrote a verse that reminds me of you,' he finally remarked.

Her brows arched in puzzlement. 'A verse? As in a poem?'

'Yes. Would you like to hear it?'

Lavera's colour darkened a shade. 'If . . . if it really reminds you of me.'

Flint sorted the words in his mind then related the words with a quiet ardour:

She walks in Beauty, like the night
Of cloudless climes and starry skies;
And all that's best of dark and bright
Meet in her aspect and her eyes:
Thus mellowed to that tender light
Which Heaven to gaudy day denies.

Lavera appeared to swallow something — perhaps it was the swell of vanity such a flattering line brought to the surface. Her lips parted, as if she would speak, but no words were forthcoming.

Conceiving her inability to reply as an awkward embarrassment, he hurried to add, 'I don't read a great deal of poetry. My father has a wide variety of books and I used to grab one to take with me when I was riding watch over the cattle herd, or to read at nights at one of the line shacks. My father is as learned as any man I have ever met.'

'You delivered that verse as if it was well rehearsed,' Lavera said at length. 'Do you often get a young lady off alone and seduce them with your practised line?'

He grinned at her suggestion. 'You are educated too.'

'What makes you say that?'

'You use proper English and I have seldom heard anyone use the word *seduce*.'

'It is not quite as *risqué* as many other terms given to a man's effort to take advantage of a woman.'

'You think it's always that way, the man being the culprit?'

Lavera removed her hand, as if realizing the first genuine advance between them had been her own. 'I was only showing a concern for your safety. You can't be suggesting that I — '

He chuckled again, this time at her bafflement, and received a sharp look for his mirth.

'What's so funny?' she wanted to know.

'The humour of this conversation,' he answered, using his most disarming smile. 'Do you always react to a compliment by starting a fight?'

'I didn't start anything.'

'You accused me of trying to seduce you,' he was quick to point out. 'I merely recited a bit of a poem and you became defensive.'

Lavera appeared ready to give him a harsh tongue-lashing. Instead, her common sense surfaced and she regained control of her emotions. 'All right,' — she grew more sedate — 'as you seem to be experienced in the area of courting protocol, what should my reaction have been?'

'A lady ought to be adept at accepting flattery with grace,' he advised her gently. 'A simple, *thank you*, or *what a nice thing to say*, would have been adequate. Being a beautiful girl, you should accept a compliment, certifiably given, without taking offense.'

'I had no idea you were a teacher of manners and proper behavior in polite society.'

'Not at all,' he responded, unmoved by the hedged sarcasm in her voice, 'but my father's position has allowed me an opportunity to witness a number of society types in action at fancy balls or the theater in Denver. I have seen some of the most attractive women in the country interact with their peers. Oddly enough, it is often the compliments from other women that seem to pose the most challenge. There seems a thin line between offering actual praise or intending the comment to be snide or mocking.'

'I suppose that is because a woman can relate to and understand another woman's intentions. She would know if the remark was meant as a compliment or sarcasm.'

'And such intuition is one of the similarities between men and women. As a man, I have no trouble seeing right though the smooth talking delivery of a gigolo, while a woman might be carried away by his every word. I guess it's natural for each gender to more readily understand someone of their own gender.'

Lavera rose to her feet prompting

Flint to do the same. She appeared uncertain of herself, nervously transferring her gaze off in the direction of the scenic view, as if purposely avoiding eye-contact with him.

'I love it here but we should be getting back. Grant isn't much of a hand at washing dishes and I wouldn't want him to think . . . ' she hesitated and finished: 'to start worrying about me.'

'It was gracious of you to share this private spot with me,' Flint told her. 'I can see why you like it. This place is beautiful, serene and solitary. A person could well sit upon your sunning rock, look out at that expanse of mountain range and ponder the secrets of the universe.'

Something in his voice or words caused Lavera to face him then. It was a frozen moment in time for Flint. He peered deep into her alluring blue-green eyes. The golden flakes which sprinkled the perimeter of the iris radiated like a shower of miniature stars, illuminating the night. He sought to probe deeper, beyond the thin veneer that protected her inner vulnerability. For an instant, he was overcome with the urge to take her into his arms and test the sweetness of her lips.

As if Lavera read his thoughts, she quickly took a sidestep and went around him. 'I must get back,' she said, her voice strangely husky.

Flint followed after her, curious as to what had startled her. Although she did not bound away like a spooked deer, she definitely did not hesitate either. As he trailed along behind the girl, he wondered how he could have handled the situation differently.

Maybe it was Byron, he thought. Should have used a more subtle quote from Shakespeare or Francis Bacon. Yep, I'll bet it was Byron who frightened her.

6

The following morning, Flint rousted Johnny out of his blankets an hour before sun-up and they rode out of town before anyone was stirring on the street.

'I thought we were waiting till tomorrow to ride down to Faro Junction,' Johnny said, once Orphan Creek was a couple of miles behind. 'Tonight being Saturday, it might be the best time to spend an evening at the tavern. A good many of the miners would be there. We might be able to pick up some information about Sandy.'

'No need putting off the ride, little brother. I want to ask some questions and look at the railroad schedule. Besides which, we can probably get a room at the boarding-house there. It would beat sleeping in that loft again.'

'That would be a shame,' Johnny

quipped. 'After I've gone and made friends with all the mice and spiders haunting the loft. I'm on a first-name basis with some of them.'

'You don't have to make the ride. I told you from the onset of this whole affair that I was willing to go it alone.'

Rather than responding to that, Johnny tipped his head up the trail. 'Camp robber,' he said. 'Got himself something to eat.' He grunted. 'Reminds my stomach of the fact we didn't have breakfast today.'

Flint observed the magpie. It was on the trail ahead, picking at a spot on the ground. As they approached, it squawked frustration at being interrupted and flew off a short distance.

'Don't see anything,' Flint said, reining his horse to that side of the path. He stopped his animal and stared at the ground.

'So what is it?' Johnny asked.

'Looks like a dried pool of blood.'

'Yeah? From what?' He stretched in the saddle and took a quick look around. 'I don't see any dead critters lying about.'

Flint surveyed the ground with a careful scrutiny. 'There are some scuff marks here — looks as if something was dragged off the road.'

'Yep, I see the footprints,' Johnny concurred. 'Maybe someone shot themselves a deer or something and then pulled it off the trail to hang from a tree limb. Could be that someone killed and skinned a buck or elk yesterday, or first thing this morning.'

'We would have heard any shots fired this morning,' Flint deduced. 'Besides, the blood has dried. This isn't fresh.'

'Can you make out any animal tracks?' Johnny asked. 'I don't see anything on this side of the road.'

Flint got down from his horse. He examined the ground and began to follow the prints. Johnny joined him before he had gone more than a few steps off of the main trail.

'What do you think?'

'You don't want to know.'

'Now, look here, Flint. We don't want to get mixed up in anything. You remember what Pa told us about not getting into no trouble.'

'*Any* trouble,' Flint corrected. 'Watch your grammar.'

'What's grammar got to do with getting into trouble? A school marm might use a ruler across your knuckles, but you don't end up drygulched from saying a wrong word.'

Flint stopped at the edge of a deep wash and peered down into the ravine. There was something down there all right, and that something bore a strong resemblance to trouble.

'Holy ham hocks! It's a body!' Johnny exclaimed, struck by the same conclusion. 'Flint! There's a man down there!'

Flint was already searching for the best route, weaving through the brush, digging in his heels and beginning his downward descent. He slid a few feet, got a second foothold and worked his way carefully down the steep bank. When he reached the body, Johnny was right on his heels.

'Oh, boy! This sure don't look good!' Johnny said woefully, poking his head over Flint's shoulder to peer at the lifeless corpse. The man was on his back, blind eyes wide open and two bullet holes visible in his chest. 'Got to be murder!' Johnny continued. 'Never heard of a suicide where the guy stripped down to his long-handles, shot himself twice and then jumped off a ledge.'

Flint used his book learning to remain objective. He studied the corpse, trying to piece together the puzzle. 'He looks to be in his mid-forties.' Lifting the man's arm, Flint gently tested the flexibility. 'From the stiffness of this here fellow and the dried blood, I'd say he was killed yesterday. The flies have been buzzing about, but there aren't any — '

'Enough said!' Johnny said at once. 'The guy is dead — he's stiff as a railroad plank and we've stepped into a hog wallow up to our eyeballs! I don't need any more information than that!'

Flint was about to release the arm, but took notice of the man's hand. He paused to examine it more closely.

'Look here,' he told Johnny, 'this guy has soft palms, but the backs of his hands are covered with old scars and busted knuckles.'

'You think he used to be a prize-fighter or something?'

'He doesn't have any scars on his face, no crooked nose from being broke or mangled ears from getting hit. No, not a fighter, but I'd say he once did a lot of hard physical work. However, it appears the man's present occupation is a different kind of job. His hair has been cut recently, he's clean-shaven, except for the moustache, and even his fingernails are clean and trimmed.'

'I don't see what that means.'

'Uncle Sandy had banged up hands like this, from getting his knuckles scraped or nicked by a hammer when working in the mines, but he had calloused palms too from using a hammer and a drill bit.'

'You said the underside of this guy's hands are soft.'

'Exactly. I'll bet this guy was once a miner, but that's about all I can tell.'

'Somebody sure enough bushwhacked him up there on the trail. Wonder why?'

Flint bent over and turned the body to expose the man's back. 'There are the exit wounds from two bullets in the chest. But see how the two holes are only a couple inches apart?'

'So?' Johnny asked.

'So he was hit on both sides of the chest from the front.'

Johnny thought about that for a moment. 'There might have been two shooters, one to either side of our guy.'

'Be a fair assumption.'

'So what do we do with him?'

'No telling how far we'd have to ride to find a real lawman, Johnny. I think we ought to take him to Orphan Creek and put it on Bullet Skinner's head.'

'He's nothing more than a hired bully, Flint. He works for the mine owners, not the state or county.'

'It's another fifteen miles down to Faro Junction. There's nothing there but a train station and boarding-house. They would have to send word for a marshal or sheriff and we'd be stuck tending the body.'

'You're right, big brother, but first things first. How do we get him out of this hole?'

'Just like a deer — you grab hold of one end and I'll take the other. We'll hoist him up a few feet at a time.'

'There might be some evidence we've missed. Shouldn't we have that blowhard, Skinner, come here and get the body himself?'

'Grab hold,' Flint ordered, not bothering to answer his suggestion. 'Looks like the trip to Faro Junction will have to wait.'

Johnny took hold of the man's ankles and stopped. 'Look here, Flint,' he said excitedly. 'The guy is missing all but his big toe on one foot. That sure ought to help identify him.'

As Flint stepped over to take a closer

look, Johnny suggested: 'Frostbite, you think?'

'I doubt it.' Flint traced a line with his finger. 'This appears to be an old scar along the bridge of his foot. I'd venture an accident of some kind.'

'It still ought to help us get an identity, shouldn't it?'

'That it should, little brother. I'd wager the guy walked with a limp. Now grab hold and let's get him back up to the road.'

It was a struggle to climb the steep hillside and take care with the body at the same time. The two brothers found it easiest to hoist the body up a few feet, take a step or two and get a new foothold, then heave him up another short way. Once to a narrow animal trail, they were able to each take an end and carry the body the rest of the way.

'Whew!' Johnny said, once they had reached the mountain road. 'I prefer dragging a deer. Hauling a dead man out of that ravine is about as hard a job as I've tackled in months.'

'Let's take a close look at the trail

before we head for town. We don't want to miss anything.'

'Hey!' Johnny said, pointing down the road. 'I see a horse down the hill — got to be our dead guy's ride!'

'There's a break for us,' Flint told him. 'Grab your mount and go get him. We might find something on his horse that will help identify this guy.'

Johnny quickly mounted and headed down the trail at a walk. He was smart enough to make a slow approach so as not to frighten the animal. He didn't want to have to chase it down and rope it on the dead run.

Meanwhile, Flint began to circle the area and study the tracks and marks on the trail. He located a place to either side of the road where it appeared a rider had waited. There were several nearly smoked cigarette butts on one side and gooey spots of a tobacco chewer on the other. He recalled the marshal liked to chew. Upon closer inspection, he detected another substance in the dried spit. If it was what he suspected, he had a piece of evidence.

Back on the main trail, he followed the markings and footprints back to within a few feet from the spot of dried blood. The two ambushers must have waited for some time, stepped out to confront the unknown man, shot him down in cold blood and headed back toward town. He was thinking the one bit of evidence would not be enough to point a finger at anyone until he took a closer look at the hoof prints from the two ambushers' mounts. It appeared one of those horses was missing a shoe.

Flint double-checked the ground a second time and made a careful examination of the trail. After ten minutes of crawling on hands and knees, he knew he was right about the missing shoe.

'She was a little skittish,' Johnny called out, having come back up the trail. 'I had to get down on foot to approach her.'

'Having the rider shot off her back is bound to make the mare a little spooked,' Flint agreed.

'Trouble is, the reins were knotted and had been looped over the saddle horn,' Johnny explained. 'The only brush the horse could eat was about knee high and she couldn't get a drink.'

'Probably the reason she let you get up to her. I'll bet she's thirsty.'

'The guy didn't have saddle-bags,' Johnny continued with his information, 'but there was a little grub, wrapped in a change of clothes, tucked under the back of the saddle. I'd say the fellow left the bulk of his belongings down at Faro Junction.'

'That's probably true. He rode up here to spend a few hours, likely not expecting to stay the night.'

'Or get himself killed,' Johnny added.

Flint walked over to the dead body. 'Lend a hand and we'll load him over the back of his own horse. We'll take him into town and give the body to the marshal.'

★ ★ ★

Bullet walked around the body, as if viewing it from a different angle would give him some special clue as to who had killed the man.

'And you found him just like this, no clothes, no gun, no identification?'

'Someone stripped his body and then dumped him into the ravine. All we found was a clean shirt with a piece of bread and can of beans tucked beneath the rear of the saddle.'

Bullet put a curious look on Flint. 'And you two just happened to be looking down into a draw and saw the body?'

'We spotted some blood on the trail,' Johnny informed him. 'It didn't take a Pinkerton Eye to see where a body had been dragged off of the road.'

Bullet sent a sharp glance at the younger Wakefield. 'Where was this again, about two miles out of town?'

'That's right,' Flint replied. 'There was a charred twenty-foot tall pine near the spot — must have been hit by lightning some time back.'

'OK, I know the place,' Bullet said.

'What are you going to do?' Johnny wanted to know.

'First off, I'll send word to Denver and have 'Old Peak' Wilcox send a federal marshal to investigate,' the peace officer answered. 'A murder outside of town ain't my job.'

Flint knew of Philip P. Wilcox. He had been a successful attorney and was once the superintendent of the San Carlos Indian reservation. He would send a qualified man to look into the death, but it would be a big help if they could identify the victim.

'Maybe you could arrange for a viewing of sorts, to learn if anyone here in Orphan Creek knows our friend. Can't be many men around with four missing toes.'

Bullet gave that idea an affirmative nod. 'I'll get word to the three mines. Most everyone is curious about looking at a dead man anyway. Fudge Jones can lay him out in the cold storage shack. We've got a little ice stored there.

Ought to keep him in good shape until the federal marshal arrives.'

'Anything more we can do?'

Bullet regarded Flint with emotionless, black eyes. When he spoke, there was an obvious hint of suspicion in his manner. 'Things have been lively since you two arrived in our fair town. You are only here to see to the burial of your uncle, but you gang up on one of my deputies and beat him up. Next, I hear rumours about you stirring up trouble at the Excalibur, claiming the cave-in which killed your uncle was something other than an accident. Then you just happen to see evidence of an ambush or murder and follow some vague tracks off the main trail and find a body down in a ravine.'

Flint did not flinch. 'And we're not finished yet, Skinner. The miners here are little better off than slaves. The company store is over-charging them on everything they sell. I'm of the opinion this town could use some kind of organization to deal with these issues.'

Bullet scoffed at the idea. 'What kind of organization would that be? The mine owners run this town and Talbot sets the prices. If these miners don't like it, they are free to move on.'

'There are changes coming, Skinner,' Flint warned him. 'A number of labour unions are already in place around the country. One of these days they will be visiting your mines.'

'Maybe you work for one of them unions already?' Bullet ventured.

Flint scoffed at the idea. 'Until I arrived here I had never seen the inside of a mine,' he said. 'Don't care to ever see the inside of one again either.'

'So quit trying to mix into something that don't concern you, Wakefield.' Bullet put his hands on his hips and thrust his jaw forward. 'You keep stirring up a hornet's nest and you're gonna get stung.'

'That sounds like a threat.'

Bullet turned his head and spat a

stream of tobacco. 'It don't have to be a threat,' he said thickly. 'Men who go around poking their nose in other people's business have a habit of getting a snootful of trouble, that's what I'm saying.'

'Sorry, but running a monopoly up here doesn't excuse murder. This man, whoever he is, was killed in cold blood and I've a hunch Shelby and my uncle's deaths were no accident either. I'm sure the mine owners don't wish to end up in court or possibly prison, so it is their hired hands who had better watch out. If I find proof to back up my suspicions, we'll see who the mine owners point a finger at.'

The threat darkened the scowl on Bullet's face. Fire came into his eyes and the muscles of his jaw tightened like a snug saddle cinch. 'Wakefield, you're about one word away from getting run outa town. Talbot, Coop and Spinner are the men who run this town. They have the money and power to sway the governor and buy most any judge or jury. You cross the line with these boys and you'll end up planted next to your uncle. You'd better think about that.'

Flint did not offer a reply, but rotated around and slowly walked away. Johnny was close by on his heels.

'Hot-dang, big brother!' Johnny exclaimed in a hushed voice. 'Did you have to go and rile him up? He'll be dogging our every move from now on!'

'I know the identity of one of the two men who ambushed our mostly naked stranger.'

'You what?'

'Yep,' Flint replied. 'I need to visit the stable and check on some horses.'

'What about the horses?'

'If I get lucky I'll find out who the second man was out there.'

Johnny whistled under his breath. 'I thought it was only me who found trouble back of every bush. I reckon it runs in the family.'

'We'll have to stay alert,' Flint warned. 'Best keep watch for any sign of trouble.'

'You want me to look at the horses with you?'

'I'll let you know what I find out. We can discuss our options tonight. I think we'd best figure on sleeping light from now on.'

'If we are going to end up facing a half-dozen guns, we had best find some friends to back us up.'

'Sounds like a good idea. Who do you have in mind?'

'I thought I might pick up a couple of things at the store and head over to the Crenshaw house. After I wangle myself a meal, I'll ask a few pointed questions and see who they trust. You go taking on the marshal and his men and we're going to need the support of the miners.'

'All right. After I check the horses, I'll speak to Fudge and Pepper Jones. They ought to know who we can trust too. If I don't see you before dark we can compare notes when we bunk tonight at the loft.'

* * *

While tending to his own horse, Flint did some discreet snooping and located a horse with a missing shoe. Some small talk and an off-hand comment to the hostler gave him the name of the horse's owner. While he was there he visited with Fudge. The blacksmith ran the forge and sharpened drill bits and the like, but he seldom did more than watch the stable when the hostler was running errands. The tombstone was nearly complete. With a little extra effort Fudge figured it would be ready to put on Sandy's grave a day early. It would be fitting to have it be placed on a Sunday.

Once Flint left the livery, he visited a few of the families, asking about Sandy and Selby, while also seeking a measure of support if trouble should come. It wouldn't be easy. Every shack showed little more than absolute poverty. The miners were trapped in their positions, suffering the stranglehold of the mine owners. The men he met returning from the mine wore long faces, the fire gone from their eyes. The few women he talked to were soft-spoken and reticent, with children who appeared thin and often sickly.

Language was something of a barrier, as the mine owners had brought in a good many imported miners, Cornish, Finns, Swedes, Germans or Italians. Those who could not speak English actually worked for less wages than the others.

After a futile visit to a dozen different shanties, Flint knocked on the door of Pepper Jones's shack. A woman opened the door and a frown of puzzlement immediately spread across her face.

'You's that lookin'-fer-trouble man, Mistah Wakefield,' was her greeting.

'Yes, ma'am.'

She grunted. 'Why is you asking for the sky to come crashing down on your head, young 'un? I doesn't wan' you takin' my Pepper with you'all.'

'Open the door and let the man enter, Selma,' Pepper said, from behind the woman. 'He's a friend.'

159

'Him be the kind o' friend what will get your name on one of them rocks up the hill, Pepper Jones. You listen to what I says.'

'I hear you, Selma,' Pepper replied. 'Now go about your work and leave us be.'

Flint entered the room far enough to close the door. Pepper looked to have just washed up from the day's work. He beckoned him to have a seat. It was something of a surprise to see that he had actual furniture, an ordinary table, but with wooden chairs, rather than stools. There was also a Hitchcock chair and a serpentine-back sofa.

'You seem to manage your money better than the rest of the camp, Pepper. I'm impressed.'

'Fudge made the table and chairs,' he explained. 'The sofa is store bought — picked it up in Denver a year back. With Fudge making some of the furniture, we do all right.'

'I don't want to impose on you, what with it being late, but I'm trying to learn the identity of our ice-house guest.'

'Swede told us miners about the dead man.' He shrugged his broad shoulders. 'I walked past and took a look inside the hut, but I've never seen him before.'

'Do you have any ideas as to who he could be?'

Pepper leaned forward. 'You got no stake in this, other than the death of your uncle, Flint. Why are you so interested?'

'I'm the nosy type.'

'Could get your head busted.'

'Bullet Skinner seems to think along those same lines.'

Pepper rubbed his chin. Unlike the other miners, he did not have a beard or moustache. When he spoke, there was an underlying caution in his voice.

'Were I doing the looking, I think I might send off a wire to Carson City over in Nevada. Seems that Sandy once said he might write a letter to a man over that way. If you look through your uncle's belongings, you might even come up with a name.'

'I went through the box of clothes and few personal items Sandy left behind. He had a notebook, but the only addresses were for my brother and my folk's place. I don't recollect him ever sending us any letters, but it listed us as the next of kin. I imagine that's how someone knew to contact us.'

'Mr Gates was the one who found the address and sent the wire,' Pepper informed Flint. 'If you were looking for any other names or the like, you might check with Todd's daughter. He might have a name or address written down some place in his things.'

'You seem to know more than you are letting on, Pepper.'

'My Pepper, he don't know nuthin'!' Selma said adamantly, pausing to stick her head around the kitchen petition.

'Hush now, wife of mine,' Pepper growled at her. 'We are talking about this man's blood.'

'It's your blood I be worrying 'bout,' Selma replied. 'You keep shed of that

162

fellow, Pepper. He's gonna get your tail-end clamped down on by a big grizzly-bear trap!'

Pepper grinned. 'Selma is a worrisome sort.'

'I don't want to put your life in danger, Pepper.'

'Your life is more apt to be in danger than mine,' the man replied. 'Talbot and the other mine owners don't like anyone snooping about. If he thinks you are going to stir things up, he'll swoop down on you like a hawk.'

'I have a hunch about who killed the man lying over there in the ice house,' Flint told him quietly. 'But I still don't have proof of the motive for his death and that of my uncle and Shelby.'

Pepper grew serious. 'I can't help you there. Sandy and Shelby kept quiet about whatever they were up to. Sticking your nose into this is likely to get you killed too.'

'Any idea who might have set the dynamite in the mine?' Flint was not dissuaded. 'What about Skinner or one of his deputies?'

'Them fellers never come into the mines.'

'Can you think of anyone?' Flint asked. 'I need to know every man who is involved before I make a move against them.'

'What kind of move can you and your brother make?' Pepper asked. 'Two of you against Talbot and his hired guns? Talk sense, man, you're going to end up buried next to your uncle.'

'I admit I might need the help of the miners,' Flint told him.

'And we would all end up out of a job and maybe get shot up as well. We've got women and children to think about.' He nodded to the kitchen. 'Our first born is due in another three or four months . . . God willing.'

'I believe Shelby and my uncle intended to get all the miners united, so they would have the power to make some major changes. The mine owners would never fire all of you at once. It would put them out of business.'

'That sounds like union talk to me,'

Pepper said. 'Best keep your voice down. The last two men who — ' He stopped instantly, as if he had suddenly realized what he was about to say.

'The last two men — maybe Shelby and my uncle?'

'I didn't say that,' Pepper replied.

'Food is on the table, Pepper,' Selma called. 'If you wants it, you best get at it afore it gets cold.'

Flint bid a quick farewell and left the Jones family. His talking to everyone had finally paid dividends. Pepper suspected that Sandy and Shelby had been trying to either contact, or form, a union. There was a good chance the dead man with four missing toes was someone they had sent for.

Flint's last stop would be at the store. Gates was the town's only telegrapher. He had been the one to wire them about Sandy's death. He would know about any mail or wires Sandy or Todd Shelby had sent out. With luck, a talk with him might allow Flint to put together another piece of the puzzle.

7

Henry Talbot sat in the corner of the tavern. He took a bite of the steak, but it did not have any flavour. He knew it wasn't the cut of meat; his taste was not for the food. With a yearning that burned deep into his soul, he watched Lavera move about the room. She was light on her feet, quick to offer a smile of greeting, and equally quick to turn aside compliments or requests to join anyone at their table.

Thinking back to his start here, it had been the sheerest of luck that Talbot had stumbled onto the two old miners at Orphan Creek. They had found a little colour, but did not have the tools or backing for an extensive dig. He purchased the Excalibur for $200, a mule and a side of venison. He had sold his family business in Cherry Creek and put every dime into the mine. Six years of his life had gone into the recovery of gold from that mine. With Coop Jacobs and Spinner King opening mines and putting up additional capital, the three of them had formed a mining co-operative and contributed enough money to put a railroad spur up the mountain. That had put an end to the slow and costly use of twenty-mule team ore wagons to haul the ore to the smelter.

He sipped from his glass of beer, his eyes following Lavera's every move. Even weary from being on her feet endlessly, she displayed the grace and beauty of a dove in flight.

I deserve someone like her, Talbot mused. He had worked so hard, missed so much. He was going to grow old alone if he didn't find someone worthy of sharing his life. Lavera could bear his children, tend to his house, prepare his meals. Once he milked all of the worthwhile ore from the Excalibur, he could sell the mine, move to Denver and live like a king for the remainder of his life. A girl like Lavera would be young enough to take care of him in his waning years.

He smiled inwardly at the thought of possessing her. Her dress was modest, but it did not conceal her feminine wares. He imagined how it would be to hold her close, to kiss her inviting lips. If only he could —

The vision was shattered when Flint Wakefield entered the room. As if there was a magnetic attraction between them, Lavera stopped what she was doing and stared at him. The two exchanged a silent greeting of endearment, before he went to a table and sat down.

A jealous fury twisted within Talbot's gut when Lavera ignored everyone else in the room and hurried over to take his order.

As if she doesn't give a red-eye bean for anyone else in Orphan Creek! he thought bitterly. Bile rose within his throat and he pushed aside his steak. What kind of magic spell had that nosy puke cast which allowed him to twist

Lavera around his little finger?

Even as he glowered at the two of them, Flint said something to bring a warm smile to Lavera's lips. Talbot was quick to discern it was not the same courteous simper she used to welcome the other customers.

He cursed vehemently under his breath. That egg-sucking interloper was stealing Lavera right out from under his nose! No sooner had he selected the choicest lady in the country for his own than Flint Wakefield had moved in to turn her head!

So consumed was he with his inner rage and enviousness, he was not aware of Bullet Skinner's approach until the man spoke.

'Been wanting to talk to you, boss.'

'So here I am!' he snapped impatiently. 'What is it now?'

Bullet pulled out the chair opposite him and sat down. He pushed his hat back with a long forefinger and leaned forward, placing his elbows on the table.

'We've got trouble — and I see you're looking right at him.'

'Wakefield?'

'The guy is a bigger nuisance than having a horde of red ants invade your drawers.'

'Lavera Shelby certainly seems to think the world of him.'

Bullet glanced in their direction a second time and snorted his contempt. 'She sure never smiled at me that way.'

'Nor me either,' Talbot complained. 'Bet if you got close enough, you would hear her purring like a cussed house cat.'

The town marshal returned his attention to Talbot and the problem at hand. 'The thing is, boss, Wakefield and his little brother found a body today — brought it in this morning.'

'A body . . . you mean *the body*?'

Bullet shook his head. 'I don't see how they found him. The body was down in the bottom of a gully. It's a wonder how they managed to find it.'

'What do they suspect?'

'A lot more than they should for being here no longer than they have! That joker over there, the one basking in the glow of Miss Shelby's affection, gave off the impression he knew who had killed the union man. Besides that, he still thinks his uncle and Todd Shelby were murdered too.'

Talbot shook his head. 'The man is getting on my nerves.'

'He's either pretty smart or damned lucky,' Bullet growled. 'We pitched the body far enough down into the gulch, we figured no one would ever find him.'

'So how did Wakefield discover the body?'

'They claim to have seen some blood on the road, but I can't figure what they were doing so far from town. Fudge is fixing up a headstone for their uncle, so it makes no sense them being that far out.'

'You did say they went to the stream yesterday for breakfast,' Talbot reminded him.

'Yeah, but Sparks wasn't out of bed

yet to see them leave this morning.'

'Who did the job with you?'

'Phelps, but he knows to keep his mouth shut.'

'I wonder if we ought to be concerned about Mr Wakefield. If he keeps asking questions long enough he might turn up some answers.'

'As far as we know, the only two who expected that guy to show were Shelby and Sandy. With them both in the ground, it should be a dead-end investigation.'

'I know, Skinner, but he still troubles me.'

'Might not be such a good idea, Wakefield being here when Murdock arrives.'

'The deputy marshal? Is he the man coming to look into the murder?' Talbot asked.

'Got the wire back before I came looking for you,' Bullet replied. 'He is supposed to be here day after tomorrow, probably Monday afternoon.'

'I don't like the idea of Murdock and

Wakefield meeting one another, Skinner. Murdock is not a great detective, but he is an honest man. If he learns of a mining accident that might be murder and puts it together with the death of some travelling bum . . . ?'

Bullet looked over at Lavera, who was carrying a plate of food to Wakefield's table. It was obvious Talbot was troubled for more than one reason. 'It's possible our friend Mr Wakefield might also have an accident, boss,' Bullet suggested. 'You know how dangerous it is in these mining towns.'

'It can't come back to us.'

'I've got an idea that ought to work.'

Talbot set his teeth, again suffering at watching how Lavera positively beamed when she looked at Flint. *She should be looking at me that way!*

He fumed inwardly yet spoke in a hushed tone of voice to the marshal. 'Do whatever it takes, Skinner, but I want no mistakes!'

'You can trust me,' Bullet told him. 'I only wanted you to be forewarned about any questions ... or incidents that might arise.'

'You're a good man, Skinner. Expect a nice bonus with this month's pay.'

The marshal stood up. 'I'll be going. Need to get a few things rounded up before it gets too late.' He grinned. 'Some accidents take more planning than others.'

'See you later,' Talbot said. Then he watched the man stride out of the room. Some of the miners looked up, but were careful not to look the marshal in the eyes. Bullet was not a man to challenge. He had been down the river and back, prison guard, railroad grunt, and had worked as a saloon bouncer in a Kansas cow town. Over the years, a good many men had felt the power of his fists or been cold-cocked by the barrel of his gun. Hiring him had been a stroke of genius.

With the marshal gone, Talbot returned to watching Lavera. She had been called away from Wakefield's table, but paused to smile at him a last time, before hurrying away to take another order. The sharing of her charm and warmth with Wakefield caused an intense gnawing within his gut.

She's never smiled at me or rushed about like that for my order, he lamented inwardly, and I own the gall-durned place!

★   ★   ★

After a somewhat edible meal, Flint went to visit the one man he had not spoken with yet. Everyone called him Weasel, the mine auditor.

Weasel was short and thin, probably no more than a hundred pounds, with narrow, suspicious eyes and a slightly crooked nose — likely once broken and never reset properly. He had obviously been in the middle of eating when Flint tapped at his door.

'Wakefield, ain't it.' The greeting was not a question.

'And you would be Ormund Wessinger.'

'Drinks all around,' he said cynically,

'we both know each other's name.'

'I won't take you from your dinner but for a minute,' Flint apologized for the interruption. 'I only wanted to ask you a question or two concerning my uncle.'

'Get on with it,' Weasel said. 'The food don't stay warm by itself.'

Flint thanked him with the bob of his head. 'Do you have any idea how those two fellows ended up with a short or quick-burning fuse?' he asked. 'Sandy must have told us kids a hundred stories of miners doing something stupid and getting hurt or killed. He preached being careful to my brothers and me ever since we were old enough to listen.'

Weasel gave an off-hand shrug. 'I would guess it was Shelby who made the mistake. His eyesight wasn't all that good any more and, when you're hammering in one of those drill bits, it raises up a thick cloud of dust. He's probably the one who grabbed a quick fuse instead of the slow burn stuff.'

Flint sighed with relief 'Thanks, that makes me feel better.'

'Anything else to make you feel better?' Weasel asked, his word dripping with sarcasm.

'Just one thing about their work. Did those two make their quota on a regular basis?'

'They was both good men,' Weasel said. 'I don't remember them ever missing their target.'

'I only asked because Sandy was always bragging that he did the work of two men.' Flint chuckled at the memory. 'Don't suppose you ever caught him loafing on the job?'

'Not him. He was a good worker.'

'Maybe he just knew when to look good,' Flint suggested. 'I mean, if he knew when you were making the rounds, he would naturally grab a pick or shovel to make a good show.'

'I never gave away my route,' Weasel said with a trace of pride. 'I like to walk softly, in case a miner decides to plop down and take himself a little nap. I often used the old trick of sticking a match in the man's boot and setting it afire.' He laughed at the notion. 'Tell you certain, that will open a man's eyes up right sudden.'

'Ouch!' Flint said, chuckling at the prank. 'Once word got around about that, I'll bet there was nobody trying to sleep when you were around!'

'You got that right.'

'Well, thanks a lot,' Flint said, sticking out his hand. 'I can sleep better knowing Sandy really was the man he claimed to be.'

Weasel shook hands, but grimaced at Flint's firm grip. Then Flint backed up a step and the man shut the door. Everything was falling into place. Just one more stop.

Flint was crossing the street when a man appeared out of the darkness. Flint clawed for his gun and stopped in mid-motion —

'Hey, stranger,' an elderly man spoke up, moving close enough so Flint could see he posed no threat. 'Would you know if they are hiring at any of the mines?'

'You a hard-rock miner?'

The man laughed. 'Is there any other kind?'

'Not in these hills,' Flint replied.

'Word reached Faro Junction that a couple of men were killed a few days back,' the man explained. 'I figure to hang around until Monday morning and ask about a job.'

'The two miners killed were from the Excalibur. Henry Talbot is the man to see,' Flint told him. 'I expect you can find him at his house Monday. It's the big place just down the road.'

'Much obliged,' the man replied. 'I'll find a place to spend the night and check out the town tomorrow. Reckon they have a Sunday meeting?'

'I couldn't say. I haven't been here on Sunday yet.'

'All right, thanks.' The fellow lifted a hand in farewell. 'I'll maybe see you around.'

Flint replied it was possible and

watched the gent wander off toward the livery. He gave his head a shake. Damn hard life moving from one mining town to another. The guy was probably on the long side of forty and had obviously walked all the way from Faro Junction.

'Flint, old son,' he muttered to himself, 'you keep after those books and finish your studies. You don't want to end up like that wandering soul.'

* ★ ★

Sparks, Phelps and Skinner all shared a small bunkhouse out back of Talbot's large house. Even though a moonless, dark night hid Flint's movements, it took him a few minutes to slowly and carefully work himself up next to a window. A quick peek told him Sparks and Phelps were sitting at a table with some cards and chips at hand.

'You hear Skinner say that Murdock was coming on Monday?' he heard Phelps ask.

'Figured he would be the one to

come,' Sparks replied. 'Not many men willing to make the trip to these distant mining towns. Murdock is one of those strange ducks who lives for the job.'

'Big Casino!' Phelps said, laying down his cards. 'Got you holding a bunch this time.'

'Damn your hide!' Sparks complained. 'You've got the same luck at cards as Skinner.'

'Skinner's good fortune at cards is not always luck, Sparks. He cheats every chance he gets.'

'And you don't?'

Phelps laughed. 'I have to cheat to compete with him.'

'So I end up sitting at a table with a coupla sharks,' Sparks lamented. 'No wonder I never win.'

Flint listened to them for an hour, but they didn't mention the man on the road or the death of his uncle and Shelby. He decided the eavesdropping had been a waste of time when he heard the cry from up the street.

'Fire!' a man's voice shouted. 'The barn is on fire!'

Flint's legs were cramped from being hunkered down for so long. He started to rise, but realized if he tried to run they might hear or see him. He quickly lay down flat against the side of the building. An instant later and the two men came racing out of the bunkhouse. Had he been on foot or moving, they would have certainly spotted him. As it turned out, their attention was up the street and they raced that direction without a backward glance.

Flint wondered about the fire, but this was an opportunity he could not pass up. He hurried into the bunkhouse and did a quick search, looking for anything that might have belonged to the murder victim. He came up empty.

Slipping along the rear of the buildings, he moved to within a short distance from the fire, within earshot of a couple of spectators. The entire barn was ablaze, flames licking at the black night sky and the crackling and power of the conflagration roared out of control. It was useless to fight the fire with a water brigade as the old wood and straw made the place ripe for burning. It was going to be a total loss.

'You hear that poor guy scream?' one short man spoke to another. 'Damn! Wish someone could have got in there to help him.'

'I seen the younger Wakefield try to go in,' the second man replied back. 'It was about the time I got here. The heat swatted him down like hitting him with a club. I tell you, that place was an inferno within a matter of seconds.'

'Too bad about the older Wakefield. He came by the house asking questions about his uncle and Shelby earlier this afternoon,' said the short man. 'Hell of a way to die.'

'If I was the suspicious sort, I'd sure wonder about him being killed in an accidental fire.'

'Old Fudge ain't never let a spark get out of hand before,' the short guy pointed out. 'You know this was no accident.'

'Maybe not, but you can bet your Sunday shoes it'll be told that way,' the other responded. 'It's too bad about Wakefield, but ain't a person here going to say so to Bullet and his pals.'

'It'll be tough on his little brother, it sure will.'

Flint backed slowly toward the shadows, not wanting the firelight to give him away. This attack had been an attempt to kill him. Thankfully, Johnny had not returned to the barn before the fire, so he was uninjured. The only possible scenario was that someone had seen the wandering miner enter the barn — he probably figured to bunk in the loft — and the killer thought the guy was Flint. Everyone now thought Flint was the dead man.

Considering his options, being dead was probably the only way he and Johnny would be safe until the federal marshal showed up on Monday. He eased back a step at a time, careful not to attract any attention, until he was swallowed by the shadows. He paused there to look over the crowd gathered for the fire and spotted Johnny. There was a girl in his arms sobbing on his shoulder! It wasn't Meg Crenshaw, the girl he had been seeing however, the gal was none other than Lavera Shelby!

* * *

It was daylight, Sunday morning, but Lavera had not gotten any sleep. She decided Talbot was going to have to go to the prayer meeting alone. She and Johnny Wakefield had stayed up all night. Once the inferno had burned itself out, the two of them, along with the Jones brothers, had dug through the still smouldering rubble to recover Flint's body. Fudge had lost most of his equipment in the fire, so Mr Gates, from the store, provided them a piece of canvas with which they wrapped up the charred corpse.

Bullet Skinner had also hung around, but he let them do the chore by themselves. He only approached to speak to them once Flint's body had been bound up for the journey home.

'Didn't lose any of the horses,' he informed Johnny, 'so both of your animals are in the corral.' When the boy didn't speak, he asked, 'You heading out this morning?'

'I'm taking my brother home,' Johnny said tightly. 'We've a family graveyard at the ranch.'

'It's a real shame,' Bullet said. 'Can't imagine how the fire started.'

'The forge is the only thing left standing,' Fudge spoke up, standing off a short way. 'I can salvage some of the tools and the stone marker for Sandy Wakefield's grave, but the bellows are ruined and most of the working materials went up in flames. There's not much left.'

'I spoke to Talbot and he has agreed the mine owners will pitch in and buy what you need to get back into operation,' Bullet promised. 'You're welcome to whatever tools and materials the company store has on hand and we can order the rest. As far as this charred mess is concerned, we can start clearing the debris tomorrow morning. With luck, we'll have you back in business in a week.'

'It will all be cleared away today,' Pepper told the marshal. 'Most of the miners have offered to help. After the Sunday meeting we'll haul off every scrap of worthless trash. All we need is the lumber for the rebuilding the barn.'

'Mr Gates has promised to place an order first thing tomorrow and get lumber shipped up here as soon as possible. He can also order the tools and bellows you need, too. This town and the mines all need a blacksmith. Yep, we'll sure take care of you, Fudge. You got my word on that.'

'You should get some rest before you leave,' Lavera told Johnny. 'You haven't slept at all.'

Johnny shook his head. 'No, I've got

to take Flint home. It's up to me to get him back to the ranch. Mom and Dad will be . . . ' But a constriction caused him to lose his voice. He blinked against the onrush of tears and walked over to get their horses.

'I'll give you a hand,' Pepper offered. 'Luckily, the saddles and tack were housed in the livery. Most everything on that side was carried out safely when they moved the horses.'

'I appreciate the help, Pepper.'

Lavera watched Johnny walking alongside Pepper Jones. She released a deep sigh and turned for her house. Her shoulders sagged beneath the weight of such a tragic loss. There was something about Flint, about the way he stirred her inner feelings, the cheer and brightness his presence brought into her world. The future was going to be dark and gloomy without his smile to lighten her mood.

★ ★ ★

Flint had remained hidden and kept watch until he discerned Johnny's intentions. Once he knew his brother was preparing to head for home, he made his way out of town and began to walk up the trail. He kept up a brisk pace and went a mile or so down the path. When satisfied no one would see him, he sat down under the shade from a squat juniper to wait. It was not yet mid-morning when Johnny appeared on the trail. He led Flint's horse with the unknown miner draped over his back. Flint felt a degree of shame for not allowing him to know he was alive earlier, but it couldn't be helped. If Talbot or Skinner knew he had survived . . .

'Pull up your horse and don't shoot me, Johnny,' he spoke up quietly, getting to his feet.

His brother had been in deep thought. He jerked on the reins and the horse following ran into his mount. The mare kicked at Flint's horse for poking her tail end and that caused the animal following to balk and dance around, nearly dislodging the body on its back.

Johnny kicked loose of the stirrups and jumped to the ground. 'Flint!' he shouted, running over to him.

Flint stepped forward to meet him — then ducked the roundhouse right hand that would have knocked him silly.

'Whoa!' Flint tried to calm him down, backing up quickly. 'Take it easy!'

'Take it easy!' Johnny cried. 'Damn your no-good hide! I lost a whole night's sleep over thinking you was dead.'

'I'm sorry about that, but — '

'And do you have any idea how worried I've been trying to think up a way to explain you getting killed? Dad would have roasted me alive!'

'You can be mad at me later, little brother,' Flint told him sternly. 'We have some work to do and little time to do it.'

'If you didn't die in the fire, who is

the poor bugger in the sack?' Johnny asked, hooking a thumb over his shoulder at the corpse.

'That's what you're going to find out. He arrived in town last night looking for work. I ran into him on the street, but he didn't give a name. I'm afraid he went to the loft to spend the night and someone thought it was me.'

'Why didn't you come out and show yourself?'

'We both might have had another accident,' Flint told him seriously. 'You have to know that fire didn't start itself.'

'Any idea who set the fire?'

'Had to be Talbot or Skinner.'

'I seen Talbot come out of the tavern,' Johnny remembered. 'What about one of the deputies?'

'No, I was watching them play cards when the fire broke out. That leaves only Bullet Skinner.'

'What're we gonna do?'

'I've a plan to turn the tables on the whole bunch.'

Johnny eventually smiled. 'And with

everyone thinking it was you burned alive, no one will be looking to stop you from putting this plan of yours into action.'

Flint gave an affirmative bob of his head. 'That's the idea.'

'So, what do you want me to do?'

'You take the body to Faro Junction. That's where the old miner came from, probably traveling by coach or train. You can backtrack his steps enough to get a name so he can be buried properly.'

'OK, I guess I can do that,' Johnny agreed. 'Then what?'

'Wait for the federal marshal, a man named Murdock. He's due to arrive tomorrow and you can return with him. I'll meet the two of you where the ambush took place and we'll discuss how to settle this.'

'A few well-placed bullets ought to handle things just fine.'

'I've an idea that might be a little safer for everyone involved. Gunfights tend to get a lot of people hurt — not only the ones who deserve it. You make the ride and try to get a name for the body. If you don't have any luck, Murdock will have to take care of it.'

'All right, big brother, but I still ought to clout you a good one. Do you know I was almost moved to tears over you getting killed?' He shook his head in disgust. 'I guess that's one positive thing to come out of this. If you get killed tomorrow I won't have to grieve over you.'

'Thanks,' Flint said drily. 'Now get going and I'll be waiting for you by that lightning-struck tree tomorrow.'

8

Lavera had managed a short nap, but it was a fitful sleep. She gave up trying when the time for lunch arrived. She prepared something for the boys then excused herself without eating. She needed time alone, time to think, time to absorb and accept the tragedy of Flint's death.

She took the familiar walk toward the woods and followed the trail to her favourite sunning rock. The place had always offered her comfort and solitude. She sought both this day, reclining on the nearly flat surface of the boulder and closing her eyes. For a time, she was able to rest her eyes, but elusive sleep was not at hand. The last time she had visited this place Flint had been with her. He had joked and teased her in a comely fashion, both with his wry glances and his flattering poem.

For the briefest moment, she had felt a spark of hope and a clandestine yearning with no name. It had been the most wonderful day she had known since arriving at Orphan Creek.

Today, however, her heart was heavy with sorrow and the warmth of the sun seemed blocked out by the black cloud which covered her. A death shroud imbued her mood, declaring the loss of something she could neither touch, nor see, nor —

'I hoped you would come here today,' a soft, familiar voice entered her world.

Lavera bolted to an upright position as if a snake had slithered across her lap! She blinked to get her eyes to focus, gasped in shock and stared straight at Flint!

'What are . . . ?'

Flint moved toward her, while quickly lifting up both hands, as if to calm her. 'It wasn't me who died in the fire last night,' he spoke the obvious. 'The body inside the barn was an out-of-work miner who had barely

195

arrived in town.'

'But you . . . you let us all believe — '
she began.

'It was supposed to be me, Lavera,'
he informed her solemnly. 'I'm reasonably certain Bullet Skinner set that fire
to be rid of me.'

'But why?' she asked, recovering her
composure. 'Why kill you?'

'Because I know the truth about
Sandy and your father,' he explained.
'The body we found on the trail was a
union organizer. All of these murders
are about the mines, about keeping the
men working for slave wages and not
giving them any kind of bargaining
power or benefits.'

'My father didn't say a word about
it.'

'I believe he and Sandy were
overheard talking about it while working in the mine. Mr Gates told me my
uncle sent a coupla wires to my brother,
Doc. He claims not to have understood
the meaning of the telegrams, but I'm
sure Sandy had asked Doc to contact

the union. They did everything right, working to get a union man up here without anyone knowing about it . . . everything except keep the secret from someone in the mine.'

'And they were killed for trying to form a union,' she deduced.

'Along with the union man,' Flint said. 'No one figured his body would be found. It was sheer luck that Johnny and I stumbled onto him.'

'And the fire?' She swung her legs about and slid off of the rock. 'You learned the truth and had to be silenced as well.'

'That's right,' he replied. 'I couldn't get word to you or Johnny before today because Skinner stuck around all night.'

Lavera feigned indifference. 'Your brother was quite grief stricken. I'm sure he was happy to see you are still alive.'

'What about you?'

'Of course, I'm glad you are alive too.'

'That's it, you're *glad*?'

She frowned. 'What else should I be? I'm relieved you weren't killed, especially if you plan to do something to help the miners and get justice for the deaths of my father and your uncle.'

Flint took a step closer. 'I thought you might have had a degree of feelings for me.'

Lavera felt her heart jump in her chest. 'You must have been imagining things.'

'OK, if you really don't care about me,' he said, keen eyes probing her defences, 'I would appreciate you not telling anyone you saw me.' And he turned around as if to walk away.

'Wait a minute!' she stopped him.

He looked over his shoulder, his expression completely unreadable. 'What?'

'Why would you think I had . . . feelings for you?' she asked boldly. 'I don't recall saying or doing anything to encourage you.'

'You're right.' He shrugged his shoulders. 'Forget I mentioned it.' And again he started to walk away.

'Flint!' And he hesitated. 'Are you playing some kind of game with me?'

'I'm sure I don't know what you mean.'

'Yes,' she said with conviction, 'yes, you do.'

Flint rotated back to look directly into her eyes. 'Tell me something, Lavera,' he said. 'Did you cry when you thought I had been killed?'

She was aghast. 'What?'

'Did you cry a few tears for me?'

'I . . . I don't remember,' she said quickly. 'It was such a shock, I — '

'Why are some women like that?' he asked, utterly changing the question. 'Why pretend you don't care when you obviously do?'

'You are being presumptuous.'

Flint moved a step closer maintaining his scrutiny. 'I have developed a genuine fondness for you, Lavera,' he told her, displaying a serious mien. 'Is it so hard for you to admit you feel the same way?'

'I . . . ' She swallowed her confusion

at such a question. 'It isn't as simple as that,' she murmured. 'You are leaving here shortly. I see no future in — '

When she paused, he asked, 'No future in what?'

Lavera could not help but squirm. 'In . . . a short, ill-advised, relationship.'

'I'm not in the habit of tasting a young lady's wares and then tossing her aside like a worn-out shoe.'

'But you didn't come to Orphan Creek to stay,' she argued. 'You will be leaving soon.'

'What if I asked you and your brothers come with me?'

Lavera was thunderstruck. 'Do what?' Her voice actually squeaked.

'Come with me to the ranch,' he said. 'Your brothers can do chores to earn their keep and attend the local school. It isn't much, but the teacher there is smart and wants the students to learn.'

'And me?' she wanted to know. 'What am I supposed to do on your ranch?'

Flint smiled. 'You would be engaged to a soon-to-be attorney at law. Once I find employment or set up a practice, you could either marry me, or seek a life of your own.'

'Engaged?' The word about stuck in her throat. 'Marry!' She was once again flabbergasted. 'I'm not even certain I like you!'

'I propose a simple test,' he said smoothly. 'Are you up for it?'

'What kind of test?'

'It takes only a kiss and you can decide if you are interested in my offer.'

'Oh, that's all!' she declared. 'I only have to let you kiss me!'

'Actually, you have to kiss me back,' he corrected her. 'Otherwise the test is not valid.'

'I . . . I . . . ' Lavera could not get her brain to function. Flint was standing right in front of her, a heartbeat away from taking her into his arms. Part of her desperately wanted to accept his challenge. But what if he was a heart-breaker, a man who lied to every girl he met? What if she gave her heart to him and he left her standing in the doorway of her cabin?

'I really do need to slip about and see some other people,' Flint broke into her mental debate. 'If you truly don't feel anything for me, say so now and I'll not bother you again.'

'No,' Lavera murmured.

Flint frowned. 'No, you don't feel anything for me, or no, you don't wish to take the test?'

'No,' she managed a bare whisper, 'I don't wish for you to *not* bother me again.'

Flint took a slow step forward, until his face was mere inches from her own. 'I would never do dirt to a lady,' he said softly. 'There is something about you that ignites a fire in my chest and makes my knees weak. Looking into your eyes is like staring at the heavens and wishing I could solve all the mysteries among the stars.'

Lavera did not respond to his enticing words. She leaned forward, lowered her eyelids and pursed her lips for the contact to come.

Flint shut off the emotional chatter and gently pulled Lavera into his arms and kissed her. It was gentle, tender at first, as if he was concerned he might frighten her. Once they had a solid seal between their lips, he allowed her to test pressure and generate her own response. As she slid her arms around his waist and encouraged a more blissful embrace, she knew she had given Flint his answer.

* * *

Johnny arrived with the federal marshal and his horse in tow a bit after the sun had peaked directly overhead. Thankfully, Lavera had provided Flint with some food, so he hadn't gone hungry.

'You're the dead man, huh?' Murdock asked, showing a natural grin. 'Look a damn sight better than me!'

'Did you learn who died in the fire?'

'The guy at Faro Junction knew him,' Murdock answered. 'We sent word to

203

his nephew and will ship his body home for burial.'

'I suppose Johnny filled you in?'

'Only what he knew,' Murdock replied. 'He said you were the brains behind solving these murders.'

Flint started from the beginning and told him every step he had taken. Once he explained about the poor miner who had died in the fire, he paused for the man's reaction.

'What about help?' Murdock wanted to know. 'You said we had five men to arrest. That might be something a Texas Ranger would do by himself — leastways, according to the writings in those penny dreadfuls some folks read — but I'm going to need a few more men.'

'I've got some help lined out,' Flint promised, climbing aboard his horse. 'When the three of us ride into town, it should get interesting real sudden.'

'All right, then,' Murdock said, pausing to lift and inspect his pistol, 'let's not keep anyone waiting.' He holstered the gun and looked at Flint.

'Your little brother here says you're hell with a gun in your hand.' He didn't wait for Flint to reply, but grunted. 'Hope we don't need you to prove him right.'

Flint put a hard look on Johnny, but he simply showed his usual smirk. He sighed with exasperation and the three of them started for town.

★ ★ ★

Lavera had been watching the trail into town. When she spied the riders she hurried into the store and notified Gates. He gave his wife a quick kiss for luck and picked up a double-barrelled shotgun. Once he was on the front porch he began to ring the alarm — a metal wagon wheel rim that hung next to the alley. It was to signal a fire, cave-in or other emergency.

As people came running from every direction, answering the alarm, Flint split off and went around the back of the store. Johnny and Murdock rode up to the head of the crowd and stopped their mounts. By the time they arrived, Talbot, Skinner and Phelps were on the street.

'What's going on?' Talbot demanded to know. 'What's the emergency?'

Gates put down the bar used for banging the wheel rim and picked up his shotgun. Fudge and Pepper Jones moved quickly through the crowd to stand at his side.

'Quiet down!' Murdock ordered. 'Everyone shut up and I'll explain what this is all about.'

Before he could do any talking a large group of miners approached from the Excalibur, which was the closest mine. Swede and Weasel were at the front. Weasel looked as if he had walked into a double jack hammer. One eye was closed and his nose had bled onto his shirt front.

'What the hell?' Talbot cried. 'Swede! What happened to Weasel?'

'He run into som'tin hard,' the foreman answered. Then raised a doubled fist. 'This be vot he run into, by golly.'

As the miners came to a halt, Murdock began to speak. 'I am here to arrest you, Henry Talbot, along with several others,' his voice boomed over the din of the crowd, 'for the murders of Sandy Wakefield, Todd Shelby and Miller Kingston, the union organizer. Also for the attempted murder of Flint Wakefield, which did cause the death of Farnnel Lavato, an out-of-work miner who died in the livery fire.'

Skinner took a step back and put his hand on his pistol butt. However, a gun suddenly poked him in his ribs. He looked over his shoulder and discovered Flint had him under his gun. Before he could try anything, Johnny moved through the crowd and disarmed both Skinner and Phelps.

'You got no proof!' Skinner shouted. 'You can't arrest me!'

'Skinner, you should never have mixed your tobacco with licorice. There were ample traces of chew left where you waited in ambush for the union organizer.' Murdock looked at Phelps. 'And your deputy's horse was missing a shoe. It was traced back to the livery. That makes him the second man who was in on the killing.'

'I have no knowledge of any of this!' Talbot exploded. 'You can't prove anything against me!'

'Weasel says different!' Pepper Jones spoke up.

'What does Weasel have to do with any of this?' Todd wanted to know.

'He gave himself away when I shook his hand,' Flint replied. 'The man hadn't done any drilling for a long time. He had grown soft from doing only paperwork. He developed some nasty blisters from drilling the hole that killed my uncle and Shelby.'

'Weasel admitted it was you who gave the order to kill Sandy and Todd!' Pepper told Talbot. 'He set the charge to kill those two men, but it was on your say-so.'

Talbot searched the crowd for support

but there was none. Skinner and Phelps were under Flint's gun. Gates and the Jones boys were all ready to pounce on him. To try and draw his gun would have meant instant death.

'Ain't no one taking me in!' a man's voice carried over the crowd.

Murdock turned in the saddle and all eyes went to Deputy Sparks. He stood at the edge of the street and had his gun trained on young Shawn Shelby.

Lavera cried out in shock, but Sparks put the gun to the boy's head. Everyone stayed back, waiting for the man to say his piece.

Johnny covered Phelps and Skinner, Fudge took Talbot's gun and covered him. Gates had a clear shot, but the shotgun would have downed both Sparks and the boy.

Flint holstered his gun and worked slowly through the crowd. He stopped in the street with some fifty paces separating in and Sparks.

'You ought to let this go, Sparks,' Flint told him in a dispassionate tone of voice. 'We don't have proof of you being involved in any of the murders. You let the boy go and you can ride out.'

'You're the one I want,' Sparks sneered. 'A big man with your fists when attacking a guy from behind. You made me the laughing stock of the entire town. Well,' he glowered, through hate-filled eyes, 'it's time for a little pay back.'

'We can drop our gunbelts and I'll give you a second chance.'

'Not this time, big man,' Sparks growled. 'This time we do it my way.'

Flint watched as Sparks holstered his gun. He then gave Shawn a shove, pushing the boy away from him. With a vicious curl to his lips and a wicked gleam in his eyes, he said: 'Come and get your due, big man. Let's see if you're as good with your gun as you are with your fists.'

A female voice shouted 'No!', but Flint was already moving forward. He had done a lot of practice with a handgun, but he didn't doubt Sparks would be faster to get his gun clear. He measured the distance, knowing most men were only accurate with a pistol from within about fifteen paces. He stopped at twenty-five. He glanced over his shoulder to make sure everyone had moved from behind him, reducing the chance of a spectator being hit by a stray bullet.

Sparks frowned at once. 'Lose your nerve, big man?'

'Draw whenever you're ready,' Flint said, squaring up to face him. 'Here's your chance to prove you are the better man.'

Sparks hesitated. To walk closer would be like admitting he wasn't up to the very challenge he had issued. He wasn't about to let Flint show him up a second time. He knew he was quick with a gun. He could do this.

Flint saw the indecision fade and the hostile rage assume control. Even as Sparks' shoulder twitched with the beginning of his draw, Flint was reaching for his own weapon.

Sparks was fast. His gun came clear and barked with sharp retorts — Once! Twice! And a third!

Flint heard a bullet whistle by his ear. Another kicked up dirt at his feet. He used nearly a full second to align his pistol before he pulled the trigger.

Sparks, after missing with all three shots, was in a near panic. He had the gun ready for a fourth round when he was hit in the chest by something hard. It didn't have the bluntness of a hammer or fist, but he realized the lead missile had passed through his body.

Hell, he thought, *can't have hurt me none — it went right through!*

But an odd numbness swept over him. The gun unexpectedly felt too heavy to lift. Sparks was trying to figure out what was wrong when he suddenly found himself looking up at the sky.

Flint's face was the first thing to block out the sun. Sparks curled his lips into a mask of hatred. 'I beat you!' he rasped, his voice suddenly lacking any real strength.

'At twenty-five paces, speed isn't what matters most, Sparks. You have to take time to aim.'

Sparks tried to scoff, but blood was choking off his wind. 'Yeah, I'll remember . . . ' he managed, 'probably be the last thing I . . . ' Then his eyes became glazed and a final breath left his body.

★ ★ ★

The following day, the marker was placed on Sandy Wakefield's grave and Flint and Johnny paid their final respects. When they got back to the jail, Murdock had three temporary deputies ready to escort his prisoners to Denver for trial. He paused to shake hands all around, before pausing to talk to Flint.

'You did a bang-up job here, Wakefield. Ever think of becoming a lawman?'

'He's not going to gallivant all over

the country risking his life,' Lavera spoke up, moving over to stand next to Flint. 'He's going to finish his law studies and become an attorney.'

Murdock grinned. 'I can certainly see why he would prefer to stay close to home.'

'If you need me to testify?' Flint offered.

'I doubt it will come to that. All of these characters have been talking my ear off, trying to avoid a noose. Won't be much to do in front of a judge other than make three of them be quiet long enough for the fourth man to speak. I suspect they'll all be convicted of murder.'

'What about Talbot's holdings?'

'Cracker will run the tavern, Gates will run the store — each of them lowering their prices now Talbot isn't taking fifty per cent — and Swede will see the mine stays in operation. Talbot has a married sister in Cheyenne. She can oversee the sale or disposition of the properties.'

Flint shook hands with the marshal and his small cavalcade rode out of town.

'I said goodbye to Meg Crenshaw,' Johnny told Flint. 'We about ready to go?'

'Soon as Lavera and her brothers get their things together.'

Lavera put a stern look on him. 'I don't remember agreeing to your proposition.'

'You do remember the test?' Flint asked.

The girl's complexion grew pink. 'Yes, of course, but — '

'I'm sorry to say you didn't pass the test,' Flint told her stiffly.

'What?' she cried.

Then he smiled his teasing simper. 'Actually, you received highest honours for the exam.' He reached out and took hold of her hand. 'I'm not leaving without you.'

Lavera rebounded quickly. 'It's a good thing I had the boys start packing.'

Johnny laughed. 'Good thing you brung me along, big brother. I'll go help her brothers get their things together. Anything to help get this travelling circus on the road.'

'Thanks, little brother,' Flint replied. 'With any luck, it's the last time I'll need you to help with our romance.'

Lavera laughed. 'I'm in total agreement with Flint. I think we'll do just fine on our own.'

THE END

We do hope that you have enjoyed reading this large print book.

Did you know that all of our titles are available for purchase?

We publish a wide range of high quality large print books including:
Romances, Mysteries, Classics
General Fiction
Non Fiction and Westerns

Special interest titles available in large print are:
The Little Oxford Dictionary
Music Book, Song Book
Hymn Book, Service Book

Also available from us courtesy of Oxford University Press:
Young Readers' Dictionary
(large print edition)
Young Readers' Thesaurus
(large print edition)

For further information or a free brochure, please contact us at:
Ulverscroft Large Print Books Ltd.,
The Green, Bradgate Road, Anstey,
Leicester, LE7 7FU, England.
Tel: (00 44) **0116 236 4325**
Fax: (00 44) **0116 234 0205**

Ward County Public Library

DISCARDED

Other titles in the
Linford Western Library:

WARRICK'S BATTLE

Terrell L. Bowers

Haunted by the past, Paul Warrick is assailed by bad memories, and in an attempt to forget, drifts from town to town finding work. But a shoot-out at a casino lands him in jail, and with the valley on the verge of a range war, Paul's actions might be the fire to light the fuse. Paul becomes involved in the final show-down — and he must not only save his life, but also his own sanity at the same time!